Prologue

I should have left them both that day,
this night that means nothing to me.]
been here, nor do I know where I am. It could be seconds, hours,
days, months. I know that I'm lonely. There's no one to talk to
except myself. If I wasn't cracked before, this should do it. If I'd
left them, would I be here now? Would this be my life? Would they
have come after me? He would. He could never lose control like
that. I remember what I did, I remember why, I just don't get what
this is, here and now. I remember the taxi. I remember the impact,
but I don't remember pain. Not physical anyway. I remember other
pain.

I can hear Axl Rose screaming *Coma* in my head on a loop.
Knew there would be an explanation. Much appreciated Axl. I
guess this means I have some kind of choice. I can stay here, listen
to my own ramblings and some golden oldies, or I can wake up. I
don't want to wake up though, I don't want to ever come back to that
world, the one that has done so much to me, has given me so much
misery. I just want to escape. Why can't there be an option of
choosing to die? Well, I have that option, I just have to wake up and
try again. Next time, maybe I should plan a little more so I don't
fuck up.

Music. That's something I remember. I love GnR, Ugly Kid
Joe, Blind Melon, Slash's Snakepit. He, HIM, he liked Oasis and
Blur. It was never going to work really. I can hear my songs now;
they are all here, not a word out of place. Suck on that Mr. I'm-a-
pretend-mod-but-really-just-don't-know-who-I-am. Evil bastard is
shorter.

I remember the face of the driver. Oh, I feel so sorry for
him. I didn't want to wreck his life too, but I wasn't thinking of
consequences. I just wanted it all to be over. Finished. I'd had
enough of 'this mortal coil'. I wish I could remember why that
phrase has a resonance somewhere. I can't remember anything

1

clearly enough, just emotions and snippets. There is pain that comes from knowing I didn't succeed. I wanted to die that day, and in a way, I'm angry that I am still thinking. It was a misguided attempt, I know that. There are easier ways of doing these things, but I was stuck. I had no choice, no opportunity, no time to find another way.

In this blackness, images flash past. It seems as though there's a reason, a rhyme, as to why. I feel like I could just reach out and touch one and the picture would become clear. Why I would do that, I don't quite know. I don't want the past, I don't want the future. I want nothingness.

I've always been a lonely person, not a loner as such, just lonely I think. I've always had people around me, but I've never let them in, let them know who I am and why I am. I keep secrets. I know that. Secrets that I shall never share. Not even with myself. I don't want that history. I want to be someone else. Someone new and not me. Someone with a different life and a different history. I've often thought of that over my life, but never had the nerve to do something about it, not until that day, when I was left with no option but the worst.

I just wanted out. You can understand that, can't you? It was my time, I'd come to the end and there was no other way forward, so I stepped in front of that taxi and wished for my life to end within seconds. Such a shame the guy's brakes worked and now I'm here, locked away. Unable to escape, unable to speak, to look, to hear, to do anything but bemoan my failure at suicide. I only have myself to blame, only myself to listen.

I wonder if the people that were there realised what was happening, or if they are now as confused as I am. I wonder what they think of me. I don't care, but I do wonder. I remember that Leanna and Bethany were there. Some guy with a video camera. The neighbours. The chauffeur for the limousine. I was there. In my wedding dress, holding my bouquet, staggering under the weight of the consequences of marriage, of the rest of my life. That's why I did it, the weight was just too much. Leanna and Bethany talked

2

about me, about what was under all those layers of white chiffon and taffeta. What a shame they didn't do anything about it. What a shame I didn't.

If I had wanted to do it, get married that is, there would have been no church, no limousine. It would've been a horse-drawn carriage and a beautiful country estate. No big pouffy dress that made me look like one of those dolls that sit over loo rolls. I would've worn my Mam's dress. I have it hidden in a box in the bank. Safe and separate. It's silk and long, slinky and sexy. My Mam really knew what she was doing when she bought that dress. Well, perhaps she didn't, as it turned out, but she knew what the wedding was about. It wasn't for covering up, like mine was, it was for showing off, for telling the world how perfect life is for you, the bride, even if that's not entirely true.

Maybe I am dead and this is that limbo. Maybe what I did was so wrong that St Peter won't let me in, but that can't be right. You need to believe in God to be able to believe in a heaven, a hell and a limbo. Another good reason as to why the Church wasn't working for me as a venue. I sound like myself. That last thought, that was me, and I know it. I can hear my voice, cynical and scathing as it always is in my head. In my mouth, it's always simpering and guilty. Never the twain shall meet. Destiny has kept them apart. I may not believe in God, but I most certainly believe in fate and superstition. Perhaps that's where I'm going wrong. No, no God could allow the things that happen on this Earth to continue to occur. A real God would've stepped in by now, like a head teacher dealing with bullies, he or she would've stepped down from on high and said, "You know what, this is seriously fucked up, now behave yourselves and play nicely before I have to kick off a plague or a flood to destroy all your bitchy little arses." Or words to that effect.

Perhaps it's the idea of fate that's wrong. Perhaps there is no karma, no good luck if you walk over two drains, bad if it's three. Step on a crack, break your mother's back. I can remember being heartbroken as a kid when out on a trip one of the other kids told me

3

that right after I'd stepped on a crack. I was devastated. They had to call my Mam to come and get me and take me home as no one could calm me down. There, that's a memory. I just wish it wasn't quite so depressing. I don't want memories, I don't want the past, I can't reiterate that enough.

I think that's why I won't grab one of these movies spinning past. Not because I don't want something to do, seriously, this is getting quite boring in here, but because there can't be anything positive there. I have no positivity. I have nothing that I want to remember, to relive, to experience. I've been through it all once, and once was more than enough, thank you for asking. It's like choosing to watch a really shit movie, even though you know it'll be really shit, but you feel it'd be beneficial to do it anyway. Like watching *Muriel's Wedding*.

I can't be dead. I am a failure. I can't have this much going on in my mind if I'm some ethereal being that is floating around in space. And anyway, I don't remember dying. I know you don't remember being born either, but I would've thought that dying would be more poignant, more important in a way. It's the time that you say goodbye to everything and so you should remember that kind of event. I just remember the taxi. Seeing the driver's face. I saw it all. Therefore, I can't be dead because I should have the chance to apologise for that.

The more the music plays, the more Axl sings, the more I am tempted by the colours. The images that whoosh around me. What will I see in them? What will come from the experience they offer? More pain? More misery? Should I bother? There's been so much already. I've had too much. Can I really face just a little bit more? I get the feeling that they're all linked up, so that once I grab one, I'll have to see them all, there'll be no choice for me, I'll have to sit through the lot. Like that time I went to the cinema with Kelly and we watched all the Terminator movies one after the other on a special screening. By the end of it, I thought we were all doomed to die at the hands of evil humanoid robots. Little did I realise how

4

close to the truth that really was. I don't know where Kelly went. She was a girlfriend of a friend of a boyfriend. Not this one, another one. I really liked her. We watched films together. I'd never had a friend before her, although we weren't really friends. I guess that's what happened to her. I moved on to the next man in my life and so lost her. I wonder what would've happened if I'd let her in? Too late now, and I'm not exactly Scrooge, I'm never going to be able to see what might have happened if my choices were different because it's too late to change those choices. Reality doesn't give you a second chance.

I'm in a coma. I have fuck all to do. I might as well give it a go. I'll just grab the next colour that comes past, the first memory. I can have a little look. If it hurts too much, I'm sure there'll be a way out, right?

I am Ruth. I am me. I am alive.

1. Ruth

She should've left them both that day.

Ruth woke up next to Fletcher. Fletch, an onomatopoeic name, connotations of retch. The smell of Febreeze mingled with that of sweat and left over Chinese as it sauntered through the flat. When Max was away on business, Ruth revelled in the brief freedom it gave her and made their home party central. That particular week she had been screwing Fletcher, he would be the next link in the chain of her life. She was playing a dangerous game, but at the time, things weren't so bad; she didn't realise how close she was to losing everything.

She watched him sleep and knew he was 'the one'. He would make her life perfect. She left him in bed to make coffee. She drank it straight from the jar because all the cups and mugs were filthy. There was only enough for one in the bottom anyway. Then, a shower, refreshing her, revitalising. She admired her svelte body as the droplets of warm water ran down. The sink was filled with vomit, but she couldn't remember how many days it had been like that. Maybe since the night of Absinth, the night she serenaded a photo of Max with *You're Pretty When I'm Drunk*. She'd become used to the smell, but it still bit through her senses that morning, there as a tart undertone to her mango body lotion.

The garden, which Max designed and worked on himself, was ruined. The flowerbeds trampled; all sorts of bodily fluids blended in the grass with alcohol and rotted food. The living room was trashed; the brand new cerise faux leather sofa Max had bought in a fit of guilt was sticky and had a blackened burn hole in the arm, maybe from a hot rock, maybe from a forgotten cigarette. She loved it when Max went away, but the aftermath of World War Three was often a little difficult to disguise. She seemed nonchalant about the whole mess. As though she didn't care, but she did. Ruth's subconscious knew what repercussions such household abuse might incur. She called in the cleaners. Whenever he went away, she told him that she had been at a health farm. He liked to think of her hanging out with other women, away from the temptations of alcohol, clubs and other men.

She returned to the bedroom and Fletch had gone. The bed was still ruffled and warm from his body, their bodies. Ruth curled up on his side of the bed and read the note she'd found stuck on the door. "Great time. Love you. Fletch x." Perfect.

She packed her bags and put a Dear John under the Charlie Chaplin magnet on the fridge. It said that she'd moved on and that it was her fault, not his; her usual spiel. This time, butterflies swooped around her insides as thoughts of him coming after her flitted through her brain, it had happened before at the end of other relationships. Only now, she would have Fletch, and he'd protect her. This time it would be different.

She stood in the porch, surrounded by a Gucci travelling set stuffed with designer clothes and waited for the taxi. Her long red hair cascaded down her back. Her gorgeous green eyes sparkled in the sunlight as usual, as they should. She checked methodically that this was true with a pocket mirror; there was always a mirror about her somewhere. It was one of her life imperatives.

Fletch had told her all about his apartment on the night Max introduced them many months previously. One of those 'aren't I fantastic' diatribes that she had a knack for remembering. He had said it looked to the north over the Thames and had views all across the city because his suite was on the top floor, he had even told her the name of the building. Before long, she was standing at its entrance surrounded by her gluttony of suitcases. A tall, handsome man with a disdainful air opened the glass doors and peered down at her.

"May I help you?" He said. He raised his right eyebrow in support of the question.

"I'm looking for a concierge for my cases."

"That would be me." He smiled, perhaps he was thinking, as she was, that she was a new resident.

"I need you to watch them while I see if my boyfriend is in the café round the corner. Thank you."

The only thing Fletch had left out when he had talked at her for a couple of hours was the apartment number, and she'd not needed to know it prior to that moment. Again, she had been in this role before. She had plenty of tricks up that puffed out Armani sleeve.

Without waiting for a reply, she walked away toward the underground car park, her Jimmy Choos clicked along the pavement. As soon as she was out of sight, she peered through the security bars, squinting to block out the glare of the sun. Fletch's MGB Roadster was parked in its bay, the apartment number large on the wall behind it. She returned to the main entrance.

"Apartment 39C please," she said, not wanting the concierge to ask any questions. She couldn't remember Fletch's surname.

"Certainly madam," he replied and led her to the lift, "I will have one of the boys bring your cases up in a moment."

"Thank you."

She busied herself by checking her reflection in the floor to ceiling mirrors. The lift smelt expensive, scented with exotic citrus fruits rather than the usual cheese and sweat. How wonderful life would be living with Fletch in such an exclusive and secure building, so safe. She smoothed down her jacket and checked her jeans for perfection. She'd put a lot of thought into her outfit for the day, it was vital, she had to make just the right impression. Clothes do not maketh the man, nor the woman come to that, but she knew of nothing else.

The lift glided to a halt and the doors opened. A female voice with a BBC accent welcomed her to apartments 39 a, b, c and d. Through the doors there was a highly polished marble floor. The communal area was luxurious with cream sofas, a coffee table displaying carefully selected magazines and newspapers along the glass surface, no tabloids, but plenty of gossip mags. Fashionable artwork had been delicately hung along the cream papered walls. It was like a doctor's waiting room in Harley Street. She'd always been such a Material Girl. She clattered her way over to Fletch's door, trying to keep her balance on the slippery surface and pressed the intercom.

"Yes?" came a cold, female voice from the depths of the wires.

She assumed it was another automated voice, as it had that same clipped accent, and so she said "Fletcher", nothing more. She should have walked away, not said anything. It wasn't as if she was completely ignorant, but the 'love you' of the note had wiped all other concerns from her mind.

The muffled sound of footsteps on a thick carpet approached the door and Fletcher appeared wearing a fabulous dressing gown that gaped in all the right places.

He looked terrorizing.

"What the fuck are you doing here?"

"Nice way to greet the lady you love."

"Who is it darling?" called the lift-lady again, but from inside the flat, she sounded real and not recorded. Comprehension silenced Ruth for a moment. From the way Max and Fletch talked, she'd always had the impression that Fletch kept his city home separate from his wife, used it as a bachelor pad. She was supposed to live in Kent somewhere.

"Why is she here?" she hissed as Fletcher called back, "A friend of a friend, nothing important."

"You need to leave. If she sees you, I'll be up for divorce." He started to manhandle her back toward the lift. She tottered precariously, clinging to him.

"But what about me? I've left Max for you."

"Did you tell him about this? Me?" Fear replaced his anger. He knew the truth about darling Maximillian. He'd spoken to her years ago. She'd deny it all if you asked though, and Fletch wasn't that interested anyway.

9

"Not yet." She tried to sound playful, tried to bring a smile to her lips and his, but her response was far too scathing and the smile snarled.

"Well go back to him and never tell him. I mean not even a hint, ever."

"Dump her for me."

She was coming across as so desperate, she didn't mean to, and she didn't like it. God only knew what Fletch thought, although, his pinching fingers on her upper arm suggested he might not be happy.

"Look, it was just a bit of fun, you knew that. I would never leave my wife. Max is my best mate for God's sake! It was a mistake, go home."

Fletcher pushed her gently away and into the lift, his fingers soft once more, but he still pressed the button for the ground floor. She watched him sprint back to his wife through the diminishing gap of the closing doors.

The concierge was waiting for her, unnervingly sympathetic.

"Come and have a sit down," he said.

He guided her into the little office behind the welcome desk. He started making tea while chatting about Fletch.

"I used to try and stop them going up there, but they always knew better. Happens about once a month. I just let them go now, keep their bags down here saying I'll send them up later and then pick up the pieces when they get back."

She registered his appreciative glance in her direction, but was too confused and unnerved by the situation, to have reciprocated. Not to mention, he was a *concierge* for crying out loud, she shuddered at the thought of losing the high life.

"Like I say, you're not the first and I expect you won't be the last."

He handed her a chipped mug that contained very sweet tea and smiled warmly as she took it.

"I'll order you a cab," he said. "Where're you going?"

She gave him Max's address, as she couldn't think of where else to go. She should have said Heathrow. She sank back in the chair, sipping the tea. She had never been dumped before. She thought that no one would ever turn her down. She had been with many "not-quite-single" men before. The ones who can go out to restaurants in certain areas of the city, but not others and only on weeknights; at the weekends they had to visit their kids from a 'previous' relationship. She had known Fletch was married, but she had seriously believed that he would choose her over his wife. They always had before. And she'd always left them for the same reason. Eventually, 'I'm sorry' wasn't good enough. The bruises and the misery stacked up and she escaped one way or another.

She came to her senses and checked her watch. It was nearly two o'clock, it would take an hour or more to get home in the late lunch traffic and she still had to unpack, make sure the cleaning was up to standard and destroy her note to Max all before he came home at half-three. 'If he finds out what I've tried to do...' The thought made her glad she had only had a cup of tea and not touched the lurid pink and yellow biscuits that the concierge had offered.

She downed the last of the tea, shuddering at the mouthful of syrupy sugar from the bottom of the mug. She hated that taste.

"How long will my taxi be?"

"It should be here any second now; I'll just get your cases."

The cab finally pulled up in the street at the front and she stood to one side, tapping her foot, while the driver and concierge struggled to lift her cases into the car. The concierge held the door open for her once everything had been rammed into the cab.

"Thank you for the tea and such," she said, and handed him a two-pound coin before getting into the car.

He laughed and threw the coin into her lap as she sat down, "I think you'll need that more than me my love."

He slammed the door shut on her confusion and the driver manoeuvred out into the crawling traffic. She could see his smirk reflected in the windscreen as he edged onto the main street.

She occupied her time by figuring out her plan of action; get home, destroy note to Max, get cases into bedroom, check through flat, start to unpack. After half an hour, when she had it all worked out in her mind, her subtle panic developed into abject terror. There were still about forty-five minutes from where the taxi currently idled to her front door; she would never make it. She had purposefully left her mobile at the flat so that Max wouldn't be able to call her.

"Isn't there a short cut or something?" she asked the driver as yet another moped sped past the window.

"No," he replied, and turned up his radio in the front of the cab. God only knew what station he had tuned to, but Tammy Wynette's *D.I.V.O.R.C.E* came blaring through the speaker over her left ear.

At ten past three, the cab pulled into the street and stopped outside the flat. The driver waited in the car and ignored all Ruth's requests for help, as she dragged her cases from the back, and broke a very expensive nail in the process. She paid him the fare on the metre and automatically gave her normal two-pound tip.

He laughed and said, "I think the same as the other bloke peaches, 'ere y'are."

He threw the coin onto the pavement and drove away. Everyone could see it but her. Ruth's agitation was written in every movement of her body, every finger tap, every swift look out the window.

She left it and took the first two cases into the flat, angry that twice in one day she had been ridiculed by minions. She tore down the note from the fridge and stuffed it into her pocket, ready for later disposal. She would flush it down the loo for safe keeping. There was only one case remaining when she went outside to collect the two she had left there. She looked around and spotted a teenage boy running to the end of the street dragging the missing case behind him. She hauled the other case into the flat, cursing the boy to hell and back, and went on a reconnaissance to check the cleaning was acceptable. All looked perfect, even the garden appeared to be reasonably similar to the way it was when Max went away.

She sat down on the sofa and burst into tears. The front door opened and closed and she heard Max put his suitcase on top of hers. He moaned softly about her going off on another little jaunt and about her stuff blocking up the hallway.

Ruth's heart stopped in her chest. He came into the living room and the cheerful smile he wore slid from his face like drool from a baby's chin. She held her breath and waited to see which of the many versions of Max would grace her with his presence.

He *was* handsome in a quirky way; he had blue eyes and brown hair, both of which were so dark they sometimes seem black. He wore thick glasses with square frames made by Valentino that constantly slid down his nose. It made him look so harmless and gentle. She still loved him. She always had and always would, no matter what.

"What's the matter? What happened?" he asked as he sat down next to her.

He put his arm around her shoulders. She tensed automatically but, he seemed to be nice Max.

She placed her head melodramatically on his chest, wiping her running nose on his designer shirt. He smelt of holidays abroad and Surf washing powder, comforting and loving smells that seemed to stay with you for life. Smells that could always be conjured up when you got out an old photo album and reviewed your personal history. Although, that was something that would never be on the agenda for Ruth nor Max. The past would always be dead for them both in their relationship. If only she'd walked away. There are a lot of 'if onlys' in this world.

"The cleaners messed up the sofa and I wanted it all looking nice for you when you got home and then when I was bringing my cases in one got stolen with all my favourites in it and then the garden looks wrong and I think the cleaners messed it…" It all came out in one whining, petulant breath before she broke back down into hysterical sobs.

"Don't get upset princess, we can get you new clothes and sort the sofa and I can fix the garden up. Anyway look what I found," he produced a two-pound coin, "it was in the street just outside the door."

There were so many times that made her keep trying, like this time, when he was so kind and loving. That's how she'd convinced herself that he could change, how she knew he didn't mean it. At that time, it was still specific. Solely related to him thinking she'd been up to something when he wasn't there to watch over her. It was still wrong, but she believed he truly only did it because he loved her, and he didn't mean it really.

She looked at the coin and felt her bottom lip start shaking uncontrollably.

"Find a penny, pick it up and all day long you'll have good luck. Pass it to a friend," he pressed the coin into her hand, "and your luck will never end. Now you have two-hundred pennies worth of good luck, and my luck will never end."

She dissolved completely into full on heart-string-pulling distress, shocking Max. He pulled her closer, his arms right around her and said, "There, there. There, there."

For once, she didn't tense up, she was certain that good, nice Max was the version that has returned from the work trip abroad. She allowed herself to hope he would be there to stay.

It never brought them any good luck, and later, she would swear that it was what brought all the bad luck. Or perhaps that was just childish superstition. Perhaps she was responsible for the bad luck. No, her only responsibility in all that went on was her own cowardice, her decision to stay.

2. Max

I watch you lying there, breathing through a tube. I caress your distended stomach, hoping that you both will feel my touch. I watch for a sign. What sign I don't know. You look so strange with no hair, and all the wires, tubes and whatnots, all your functions recorded and on display. All the bruises I gave you slowly fading, but not the questions that go with them. What should I do? How can I make you better? Why won't you open your eyes Ruth? Why did this happen?

I keep saying to myself, over and over again, look Max, look what you did. But it doesn't really sink in. It's like, it's a nightmare. It's a nightmare that doesn't end. Every time I feel like I'm moving on, and just thinking about getting you better, another nurse comes in and shifts the blanket. When that happens, I see the bruises once more and it reminds me of what I did. I'm a man. I shouldn't have ever done this. I guess I just couldn't talk. Now, I have plenty of time to talk to you Ruth, I just don't know if you can hear me.

I know that I treated you unfairly and that I didn't look after you the way that I should have, but even so, why? I loved you, I just couldn't cope with you. I gave you everything I could to make you happy, but it wasn't enough, was it? I was never enough, and so I had to prove to you that only I could love you. That we were meant for each other and no one else.

And now, here you are, lying there, trying to breathe, trying to live and nothing that I do will make you do those things. Keep fighting Ruth, I'm here too. I'll always be here. Always by your side.

3. Ruth

A few days later, Max called Ruth from work to say he had finally
managed to get them a table at Fifteen for dinner. She was ecstatic;
he had been trying for months at her insistence. It had been so
difficult to get a reservation there, she was utterly desperate to go.
She wanted to use the evening to make it up to Max, without hinting
at what she had done. Guilt gnawed at her, but honesty would have
been suicide. She took a long hot bath and dressed divinely. She
planned to start the evening by being eye candy and end it by being
his candy. Max came home from work in the early evening and
surprised her with a beautiful white gold diamond necklace and
matching earrings.

  It was as he fastened the necklace around Ruth's neck that
she did it. His hands brushed against her shoulder blades as he
dropped them from her neck. Her shiver of fear couldn't be
disguised as anything else. His hand clamped around her upper arm
and he spun her around to face him. The back of her head crunched
against the mirror, slivers of glass trickled down her dress and
scratched her back. She could only think that she would have to
replace the mirror in the morning. He would be even more angry if
she didn't. First, she would have to face this punishment. She had
learnt to relax every ounce of her body in such situations. It made it
less painful later on.

  "What was that for?" he screamed into her face, his teeth
millimetres from her nose.

  She didn't respond. She knew better than that, but it was
already too late. He punched her in the stomach. He didn't hold
back. It felt as though her diaphragm was squeezed into a golf ball
and couldn't burst back out into a normal position. She couldn't
breathe. She doubled over, trying fruitlessly to haul air into her
lungs. All she could see were his bare feet walking away.

  "One day you'll learn," he muttered. And she did,
eventually.

It took very little time for Ruth to recover, she didn't even cry anymore.

When they arrived at the restaurant Max had to park a good five-minute walk away. He dropped Ruth off at the doors while he took the car to a space. She sat at the bar of Fifteen, waiting for him to return. She kept her eyes lowered and didn't order even so much as a drink. She knew that what happened earlier was her fault for not being grateful and Max had forgiven her now. All was well. But just to be safe, she wouldn't engage anyone in conversation or draw attention to herself. She would just wait in silence.

When Max finally returned, she was then able to eagerly watch the people in the kitchen, reflected in the mirror behind the bar. She hoped for a glimpse of Jamie Oliver. Perhaps he would see her, read something in her face and take her away. But no, such dreams were childish. She focused on Max and her love for him. She was in heaven as she sat down on the pink padded bench seat on one side of the table and Max slid into an elegant curvaceous white chair opposite her.

She smiled at him and furtively glanced around the bustling room. She had wanted to go there since the day it had opened. It had been the one thing she had braved hassling Max over. He had been good natured about it. What he did not know was that it was her hope that she would be spotted by someone rich and famous. Someone benevolent. She'd always felt that Fifteen would attract that kind, the right kind, of clientele.

"Just like being at home," Max said. The bench seat was exactly the same colour as their sofa.

"I told you I had good taste," she said, trying to keep his good humour going.

He reached across the table to take her hand. She flinched as their fingers met. He grabbed it as though it was unbreakable and yanked it back across the table to him. She felt separated from her own hand, a wall she'd built, just in case.

"I love you for it too," he said and kissed her knuckles, traces of his spittle glistened on her skin.

Perhaps he didn't notice her reaction. There was a squirm of anguish in her nether regions. She gave him a vacant smile and continued to sneak glances around the restaurant to see if she could spot any celebrity diners.

They whiled away the wait for food discussing Max's week in Antigua. Ruth's only comment was that Max's tan looked good on him then she switched off to his monotonous rambling. Her mind was elsewhere, thinking about Fletch and revenge; thinking about being alone with Max later. She controlled the shudders this time, although, as she was wearing next to nothing, should he have noticed, she could have said that she was just feeling a little chilly.

The first course arrived; she had chosen the signature dish of scallop crudo and Max had ordered venison tartare with black truffle.

"Oh the presentation, it's just so exquisite," she said, genuinely excited by what had been placed in front of her.

"My dear, it is sustenance, not art."

He laughed at his little joke; Ruth smiled along too and played the game. They swapped morsels of their starters and squabbled amiably about which was better. The evening was so lovely; Max was back and every single second spent in his company counted. Every millisecond proved he had changed.

The maitre d' sat a couple at the table next to theirs. Ruth didn't see; her eyes were closed, play acting enthusiasm for Max's truffle. Her eyes were always closed.

"Fletch, Leanna, how good to see you! Isn't this a surprise!" He was never destined to be an actor really. Absolutely no natural talent.

She opened her eyes and shot the filthiest look she could muster at Max before turning to greet Leanna and Fletcher. There were times when Ruth made the effort to stand up to him, but they were too few and far between, mainly because the repercussions

18

were just so painful. She'd never met Leanna. She was beautiful, tall and dark. 'She *could* do with losing a few pounds and some Botox along her brow wouldn't go amiss either,' Ruth thought.

She greeted her and turned to Fletch, who had sat next to her. He gave her one of those secret winks perfected by the dirty old men wearing trench coats you sometimes see meandering around the public parks of London, or any major city for that matter.

"Hi Ruth," he said, as though nothing more than a casual acquaintance had occurred between them.

He held out his hand either for her to shake it or for him to take hers to kiss it. She might've thrown up immediately had it been the latter, as it was, she didn't get a chance to find out.

"Nice to see you again."

She inadvertently spat chewed up venison and black truffle over his hand and the cuff of his Armani suit. He grimaced and used his napkin to wipe off the gritty substance.

They chatted about holidays they had taken and were going to take, cars the men admired and the terrible price of housing as they ate their meals. He and Max had obviously pre-arranged this meeting. Max's greeting when they arrived had said it all. Ruth endeavoured to ruin Fletch's evening, just as he had ruined hers with his "unexpected" arrival, and the acting that she would have to do to keep an even keel.

This did not stop her from playing her games. She successfully knocked over Fletcher's wine as she stood up to go to the bathroom halfway through dinner. The red stain-to-be neatly poured over his plate and slopped into the crotch of his cream chinos with bits of leftover food. Max was so embroiled in talking about Antigua that he, thankfully, appeared oblivious to Ruth's intentions. Fletch seemed to pick up on what was happening. When he could get away with it, he glared at her and mouthed insults. When they had finished, Max suggested that they all went to a bar for a nightcap.

19

"I can't, got to pack for America tomorrow morning," Fletcher said.

A frown furrowed Leanna's face. "But sweetie, I've already packed and your flight isn't until five in the afternoon, so…"

"And I have loads more to tell Leanna about Antigua," Max said.

Maybe it was because she was a more willing audience than Ruth, but just maybe it was because he was ready to move on too.

Fletcher looked disgruntled; Leanna smiled at Max flirtatiously, which got Ruth's hackles crawling.

"Ok, but we should get nearer to home, Digress City?" Fletcher pointedly asked Max.

"Perfick," Max said.

They separated and drove down to the boys' usual haunt. The two men became ridiculously drunk very quickly and spent the rest of the night slurring about football. Leanna and Ruth stuck to mineral water and talked politely about clothes and shoes and celebrity gossip. Inane banter: the expected conversations. She asked when Max and Ruth planned to tie the knot. Ruth changed the subject.

Occasionally, she'd sneak sidelong glances at Fletcher, trying to see if he was watching her, or listening at all to what she was saying. Unfortunately he was too drunk to do anything much except argue about Arsenal and Chelsea with Max. When time was called, Leanna and Ruth simultaneously sighed with relief, although she assumed it was for different reasons. They said goodbye hurriedly outside the bar and dragged their men back to the cars. Ruth bundled Max into the passenger seat and took off her stilettos to drive. She chucked them into the back seat and almost took his eye out as they flew over his shoulder.

"Have I upset you?" Max asked after the first few minutes of awkwardness.

"No," she replied in a tone that lent itself to making him feel paranoid. This was so stupid, but spending so much time with Fletch

20

that evening had made her reckless. 'Fuck it,' she thought, 'what was the worst that could happen?' Although she knew the answer to that question, she still carried on baiting.

He looked suitably worried for a while but he couldn't manage to beat the booze and dozed off. As she drove, she played through in her mind the very few moments when she had seen Fletch looking at her. She tried to decide if they had been jealous, leering, just interested or completely uninterested looks. She was still obsessed. Obsession. Depression. She was falling to bits all the time.

She drove down their road and as usual at that time of night, there weren't any parking spaces in sight. She finally found one three streets away, but she had to stop the car in the middle of the road to remove a wheelie bin before she could park. Fuming, she reversed Max's brand new BMW, not concentrating as she muttered to herself about the wrongs of not being able to park outside her own home and people's lack of care about where they left their bins. She was so wound up that she backed his car into the one behind, setting of its alarm, waking Max up in the process.

"Wha' wa that?" he said, stifling a yawn.

"Nothing," she replied innocently as she brought the car forward the required six inches and pulled up the handbrake. "We're home, well, as close to home as I could get us."

As she reached into the back and salvaged her Guccis from the debris of McDonald's Drive Thru wrappers, she thanked all the gods she'd ever heard of for letting her get away with that one. Max ambled around to where she stood locking up the car and flung his arm around her shoulder.

"Carry me home babygirl," he said.

Again, what was the worst that could happen? Again, she knew, but perhaps that knowledge was what subconsciously made her push. That night, she was really beyond caring. Her dreams had been shattered and she was facing up to a life she wasn't sure she truly wanted.

21

"No," she snapped and stormed off as fast as strappy sandals could carry her. That was the first time she had ever out and out said no to him. Maybe when they first met, she might have been stronger, but she doubted that. If she'd been stronger, he would never have dated her for more than a week. He liked women that were subservient from the get go. Max didn't say anything, he just followed her. At the end of the first road, the heel snapped off her inappropriate-for-stomping footwear and she tumbled to the kerb.

"Are you alright?" he called, running up like a retired Baywatch lifeguard.

"Do I look alright?"

She really was coming to the end of her tether that night. Her stomach was bruised and sore, she suspected that eventually he would kill her. She had got to the end, almost. If only she'd kept up that strength and left there and then. But here we are again, back to the 'if onlys'. Love conquers all, or so she'd heard people say.

"Come here," he said, and bent down to help her up, giggling at her drunkenly. She couldn't see what was so funny. "Let me give you a piggy-back."

She resigned herself to the fact that he would probably carry her home in a fireman's lift if she said no to that, so she climbed onto the nearest garden wall, flung her arms around his neck and he lifted her off. He serenaded her with Oasis' back catalogue all the way to the flat, out of tune and forgetting half the words. She didn't tell him to stop. She loved the way he sang to her when he was drunk. He almost dropped her as he tried to unlock the door, but he refused to put her down. He bumped her head on the wall a couple of times as he bounced from side to side down the hall. He carried her into the bedroom where he deposited her on the bed like a sack of potatoes. He immediately passed out on his side without another word. She lay awake for a long time.

A cold cup of tea on the bedside table told her she'd overslept. There was a note propped up against it: "Love you. Max. xxx"

22

The similarity between his note and Fletch's did not escape her, but before she could think anything more about it, she was hurtling out of the bedroom and into the bathroom where she was violently sick. She lent her head against the cold Spanish tiled floor and took a deep breath. She hadn't been sick for many years. She stood up slowly, flushed the toilet and went back to the bedroom clinging to the wall for support. She was supposed to be meeting some of 'the ladies who lunch' at twelve-thirty, but at that moment, she felt like she never wanted to eat again. She found her mobile amongst the junk on her dressing table and sent a text to them all saying she couldn't make it because she was ill and then went back to sleep.

An hour later, Max called.

"Hi honey, I just had an e-mail from Marcus, he said he called Bethany earlier and she said you were sick so couldn't go to lunch with them today, are you ok?"

"I feel a little better now that you've woken me up," Ruth replied.

"You're not pregnant are you?" he asked, trying to hide his amusement.

"Of course I'm not. I always take my pill like a good girl. I've been off colour for a few days. Or did you not notice?" She was tempting fate really, but in the front of her mind, was yesterday's punch.

"Oh… erm… well… I'm sorry? Look, text me later, and if you're feeling better I'll bring home a take out with me, ok? I know you're not pregnant, it was a joke, honest."

It was so unlike him to be so kind, she felt a tingling of unease in her subconscious, but then again, she often felt like that when he was nice. It made her wonder when the change would happen next.

"Ok."

She put the phone down and lay on her back, staring at the ceiling until she couldn't see the cracks anymore because her eyes

23

were so unfocused. She wasn't on the pill. She never had been. She had never seen the point. Max always used a condom, as far as she was aware, she never usually paid much attention, it was all about getting it over with for her. Condoms were his department. Did she use a condom with Fletch? She wasn't entirely sure. The first night they had sex, she had been very drunk and fairly stoned. It was kind of frenzied, not a lot of thought had gone into being careful. She started to sweat. It felt like she should be writing lines, 'I must not be pregnant' as atonement for being so naughty, or stupid, or both. She rolled over onto her stomach and buried her head in the pillow, berating herself for being so reckless.

She needed to take a test. She hurried to the nearest chemist and bought the most expensive one. She didn't want Max to be at home when she got the result. She wanted to find out for herself first of all, and then tell him when she was ready. If she ever told him, that was. Blurred images of abortion flashed through her head as she walked to the public toilets in the park.

She took the test in a cubicle with various lewd propositions inscribed on the walls. The rancid smell of ancient urine and salty semen, heightened by the early summer heat, was almost too much to bear; it made her nauseous again. Taking shallow breaths through her mouth, ignoring the used condoms and needles littering the floor, she managed to wait. The result came and it was negative. She was ok. The relief that flooded through her was amazing; it felt like a hit of clean cocaine. She sent a text to Max and asked for Chinese food, her favourite, and then put all thoughts of pregnancy out of her mind.

When he arrived home, there was no furniture in the lounge, she'd given it to charity, leaving only the electrical goods that looked forlorn on the floor without their stands beneath them. Even the sofa had gone. He looked around the empty lounge, amazed and confused.

"I'm decorating, we'll have to sit in the kitchen to eat." She beamed at him, expecting him to be pleased with her announcement.

"But what was wrong with it before?"

She felt the tension building. She didn't want another evening ruined because she'd done something stupid.

"Nothing, I just wanted to show you how grateful I am for the jewellery that you bought me, and the dinner at Fifteen. I felt I should make more of an effort in our home."

She was sitting on the floor in the middle of the room, her hair in a loose knot on top of her head, in her imagination, she looked stylishly wild and sexy. She was even wearing the problematic earrings and necklace. She was an island in a sea of interior design magazines, colour charts and furniture catalogues. Of course, part of her was already afloat; the mooring had drifted. The carpet was covered in pages torn from various sections and then put back together in colour-coordinated groups so she could assess which schemes worked best.

Max shook his head, smiling. "Come on, let's eat it while it's hot."

She followed him into the kitchen, a colour chart still in hand, relieved that the moment had been diverted, peace reigned once more. In her thoughts, she believed Max had finally made that often promised change, that he finally had control over his temper.

She poured the wine while Max sorted out the meal. They sat down in the breakfast nook to eat the food. Ruth's good feelings returned slowly while they gossiped about their friends. She only had to stop worrying about Fletch and she would be fine. She knew she was not with child as they said in polite company and that was all she really wanted. She didn't ever convince herself entirely, but she did try.

After dinner, she showed Max swatches of colour that she thought would look good and would have the right contrasts and effects for the room. They went through the catalogues, Ruth showing him the furniture she planned to order. They cuddled up together silently in bed that night, and there was no awkwardness to the stillness between them for once.

He kissed her temple, "I would be happy if you did get pregnant, just so you know."

"Maybe one day we'll have to forget the protection," she replied and turned her head to quieten him with a sultry kiss on the lips. She always remembered that kiss distinctly. It was the way she had always imagined the first married kiss at the altar to be.

4. Little Ruthie

The little girl sat at the white Formica table colouring in her picture of a Princess. She liked to think it was Cinderella in the picture, just as she liked to think she was secretly Cinderella and someday a Prince would save her too. All Princesses were Cinderella to Ruth, even Princess Diana. The weak sun streaming through the kitchen window glistened through her fine strawberry-blonde pigtails from. Behind her, laid unconscious on the floor, was Mam. A large woman who looked strong, but someone had quite clearly been stronger. She had vivid dark hair with a bruise to match forming on her temple. She was laid on her stomach where she had fallen, her blackening profile slapped by the same sunlight that drenched the little girl's hair.

Ruth coloured quietly. She knew Mam was asleep on the floor. Father had said, "Mummy needs the rest," when she'd tried to ask him.

To Ruth's ears, it was a strange rest. Normally her Mam snored, she could make words out of, and even have conversations with, the strange, deep noise. But at this moment in time, she could only hear her Mam breathing slowly and deeply; there were no grunting noises coming from her.

Today had been a bad day. Mam and Father had been in the kitchen putting the shopping away. Ruth had been given her Princess colouring book and a new pack of Crayolas because she had been so good while they were in the supermarket. Father had told Mam off for buying posh toilet rolls, Mam had laughed saying she didn't want to wipe her bottom with newspaper cuttings. She kept on answering him back with joke answers, and Father had got more and more snappy. Then Mam had thrown a Marathon bar at Father, telling him to "lighten up." She was still laughing.

"I'll give you lighten up, bitch," he replied.

He hit Mam all over her, punching her over and over again as if he were a boxer in a heavyweight title match. She had screamed and cried, raising her arms to cover herself, trying to protect herself from the onslaught, unable to fight back against his anger.

"Not in front of Ruth. Please!" she shouted at him.

Finally, Father had made Mam go to sleep. From the crack in the door of the cupboard under the stairs, Ruth had watched him leave the kitchen. She hid in there with the mops and the dustpan and the electric box until it was all quiet again.

Ruth finished her picture. She had worked really hard at colouring between the lines and not scribbling because that always made Father angry. She picked up her picture wanting to show it to Mam, but she was still asleep. She took it into the living room instead where Father was in his chair watching television. He was smoking a cigarette. The bit of his first two fingers between the bottom knuckles was yellow. He had a light brown beard and that was yellow too in the right hand corner above and below his lips. Ruth hated beards, they reminded her of clowns, and she was frightened of clowns.

Ruth took her picture to the arm of his chair, holding it in both hands like it was a shield. She did not speak because his face was still red; she waited patiently. After a few minutes that felt like forever, he shoved her hard in the chest without looking at her, sending her sprawling onto the carpet. The picture was torn in two. Ruth did not cry because he might really hurt her if she did.

Ruth made herself very small so that if he should chance to look at her, she would be so small he wouldn't see her. She crawled from the room, a piece of the picture in each hand. She continued to crawl all the way to the kitchen where she placed the two halves of the picture together next to Mam's face. She wanted Mam to see the picture the second she woke up. Ruth curled up like a cat and nosed her head beneath Mam's arm. Then she lay there silently waiting for her to open her eyes.

After what felt like ages, when the only light was the orange glow through the window of the street lamp, Ruth fell asleep. Her Mother had still not woken, but her breathing had changed. Now it

28

was the normal snoring that Ruth was used to, although it sounded a bit distorted through her broken nose.

Weeks passed and Mam's face became the yellow of the daffodils in the garden instead of the black and purple winter pansy it had been. Mam had even stopped slurring her words so much.

Father had returned to work not long after Mam's sleep. He had been full of apologies in the final few days before he left, but Ruth hadn't believed him. When he was around she hid in the cupboard under the stairs. She knew he was due to return once more in a few days' time. He had phoned them from Abroad, drunk and sober. He always told them that he loved them and that when he got home things would be different. She had searched for truth in his words, but found them empty. When he had drink inside him, he would call and promise the world and its treasures. At these times, he called Ruth his "little Princess". She was even more disbelieving of what he said in these calls than she was of his sober conversations.

Ruth knew he worked in a hot country because when he was in a nice mood, he would tell her about the desert sand and how it stuck in his throat. He would gargle Listerine in the bathroom and show her the sand grains in the orange mixture as it ran down toward the plughole.

Ruth was nearly ready for big school and so Mam had been teaching her new things. She could read a picture book by herself and write her own name. Mam had taught her how to check off the days on a special calendar so she could tell when Father would be home. She couldn't tell Mam that she did this with terror rather than joy as the amount of days to be crossed through grew smaller, but sometimes, she thought that perhaps Mam knew.

Mam always spent the last couple of days before his arrival sprucing up their home. Ruth had sat at the kitchen table chatting while Mam emptied each cupboard in turn, scrubbed inside, laid down a square of wallpaper on each shelf and then refilled it with whatever bits had come out from it in the first place. Ruth watched

29

as she washed down the living room walls and cleaned the carpet with vigour.

"Daddy might let me decorate when he gets home. I really think he has changed this time," Mam said.

Ruth brushed her doll's hair and said nothing. Her doll was dressed as a Princess and she didn't think Ruth's Father had changed.

The day came that he was due home; Ruth dutifully crossed the "number one" from her calendar. She sat by her bedroom window using the ledge for her My Little Ponies. From there, she could see the length of the road and the people in the allotments opposite. Every time she heard a car coming, she surreptitiously looked up the street, Butterscotch still jumping the fences with her distracted hand. Mam came up at ten or so and asked if she wanted some elevenses, as she hadn't touched her breakfast. Ruth refused and continued to play. Mam came up again at lunchtime and left sandwiches and crisps, which were still untouched when she came up to ask what Ruth would like for tea. Ruth didn't want tea; she was too busy at the gymkhana.

When darkness fell and it was bedtime, Ruth asked Mam if she could stay up until her Father came home. She agreed, on the condition that if it got too late, Ruth would go to bed quietly. Ruth stayed by the window until she became too tired to watch anymore. Even her favourite fire engine red dungarees that she had especially worn for his homecoming were tired. She called Mam to say she was ready for bed. Mam came to tuck her in and said that maybe they had got the day wrong and her Father would be home the next day. After Mam had returned to her own vigil downstairs, Ruth got out of bed and knelt by her Old Woman in the Shoe night-light. She prayed to God to thank him for keeping her Father away, and then she got back into bed and slept soundly.

The next day and the next, her Father didn't come home and didn't telephone. On the fourth day, Mam made her put her dungarees out to wash because they were getting smelly. Ruth also

30

ate a chocolate digestive. Lemondrop began her chance at the gymkhana and when she was finally groomed for her tour of the jumps, Father called. She heard Mam answer the telephone to him and so she crept to the bottom stair to listen.

"Where are you?" asked Mam.

"When are you coming home?"

"Why didn't you call earlier? I've been so worried."

Each time she spoke, silence filled the space before she spoke again. Ruth tried to imagine what her Father might be saying in these gaps and almost wished she could hear his words.

"Will you be home next time?"

"What should I tell Ruth? She's been waiting for you every day and she won't eat."

This was broken up by the longest quiet yet. On the stair, Ruth watched dust dancing through the air in front of her eyes. She could hear the tinny sound of her Father shouting, but still not his words.

"I'm sorry, I'm sorry," Mam spluttered her apology for another thing she hadn't done. She came to the bottom of the stairs and started when she saw Ruth sitting there.

"Ruth, Daddy's on the telephone. He'd like to speak to you," said Mam.

Tears were dripping from Mam's chin and onto her big bosoms, leaving dark patches on the blue cloth. Ruth watched Mam's face for a moment, looking for a sign of what she should do, what she should expect when she spoke into the telephone. There was misery in Mam's face, but nothing unusual, she went to the telephone and said hello.

Father spoke, "Hello my little Princess, why aren't you eating again? Is it Mummy's cooking? I can fix that."

"There's nothing wrong with Mam's cooking, but I'm very busy with the gymkhana I'm afraid. Can you call another day?"

She didn't like talking to her Father when he'd been drinking, the slightest thing could make him mad at her. Her Father was quiet for a moment, and then when he replied, he sounded like there was a fish-bone stuck in his throat.

"I'll let you get back to the horses then. Say goodbye to Mummy for me."

"Goodbye."

Ruth put the phone down before he could say anything else. She gave his message to Mam and returned to her room. At teatime, Ruth came downstairs and ate pizza and chips from her lap in front of the television. She knew Mam was still sad, but she felt very happy.

Mam made her a new calendar to prepare for Father's next homecoming. Ruth had dutifully marked off all the days and in the space for the following day, Mam had written "sixteen-thirty". Mam had explained that this was twenty-four hour clock and so it showed that Father would be home in the afternoon. Mam had washed and ironed Ruth's red dungarees especially, although they weren't her favourites anymore and they were starting to become a little uncomfortable because she had grown. Mam cleaned again, and Ruth refused to eat.

"I'm just not hungry," she told Mam.

Mam pursed her lips as she looked down at Ruth.

"If you don't start eating soon then I'm taking you to the doctor," Mam said.

"But why? I just don't feel hungry today, the doctor can't make that better," she replied.

"He can," Mam said in a tone that told Ruth that this was her final word on the matter. She thought that the fact Mam had made a threat instead of actually taking her showed Mam might just have understood why she wasn't hungry.

This time, Ruth decided to build a wall to keep her safe. Mam continued to say that Father had changed, but she was not going to take a chance. She got all the books from her own cupboard and those from Mam's room and started to build the wall between her bed and the bedroom door. Mam was able to step

32

neatly over it when she came to tuck Ruth in to bed. She knew though, that by sixteen-thirty the next day, she would have built a wall big enough to keep her safe.

She worked all the following day until six in the evening when she could no longer reach the top of her wall. Mam came in to ask her what she wanted for tea, but Ruth still wasn't hungry and her Father still wasn't home.

"I'm sure it's just the traffic, he'll be here soon," Mam said.

At nine, Mam came in and put Ruth to bed, saying it was late enough. Mam switched on the Old Woman in the Shoe night-light.

As she left, she said, "I am sure he will be home this time Ruth, maybe I got the time or the day wrong."

Ruth knew that it wasn't the traffic and that Mam hadn't got anything wrong. Mam had said the same things before. She prayed again that her Father wouldn't come home at all, as that had worked the last time. She shut her eyes and dreamt of playing sandcastles with Mam on a beach.

She opened her eyes to the sound of the bell. She felt cosy and safe in her nice warm bed, but something she had forgotten had awoken her. She began to think that maybe she needed to use the toilet and then she heard the bell ringing again. It was the same kind of bell that you get on a boat, but they had it as a door bell. Mam loved it and polished it every Sunday. Ruth still couldn't reach the rope to ring it without being lifted up, but she was nearly there. The bell was still ringing, the caller shaking the rope incessantly. Father had come home.

She slipped out of bed and tiptoed to the window to peer out. It was very dark, so Ruth thought it must be very late. She couldn't see the front door, as it was the opposite side of the porch to her bedroom window. She heard Mam open the door and Father started before it had closed.

"You stupid fat cow, why the fuck did you change the lock?" Father shouted.

Ruth couldn't hear Mam's reply, but she knew that Mam hadn't changed anything on the door. Mam's screams started to fill the house from the hallway, as the heavy wooden front door was slammed shut.

She heard Mam say, "Please don't, you'll wake Ruth, you promised." But the roaring and crying and screaming continued.

Ruth walked slowly around her wall of books and closed her bedroom door as quietly as she was able. She got her too-small dungarees and stuffed them along the crack at the bottom of the door. Making herself as small as possible, she crawled back around her wall and climbed into bed. She curled into a ball and pulled the duvet over her head so no one would see her. Thunder trembled up the stairs and lightning crashed open her bedroom door, turning the darkness behind her closed eyes red.

Books flew through the air as her wall was bombed apart. The Old Woman in the Shoe had her home split in two by Ruth's book of Children's Prayers, the bulb that kept the children warm exploded into tiny shards. Father pulled back her duvet. He grabbed her by her wrists as she tried to cover her eyes so she wouldn't see. He punctuated his speech by slamming her down on the bed and yanking her back up again, to throw her back down on the next word.

"Why – are – you – awake? What – are – all – these – books? You – are – a – horrible – little ..."

Mam stumbled into the room. Blood was running down her chin from her mouth and her left eye was red where it should have been white. She limped as though something somewhere inside of her had been broken. Her face was screwed up in rage. She grabbed Father by the shoulder just as he had thrown Ruth down on the bed once more. She dragged him back, and launched him with all her strength against the bedroom wall.

"Not Ruth, never Ruth," she shouted.

She saw the look of shock and guilt on Father's face. He stared at her in confusion and moved his hand toward her gently as if to touch her, to comfort her.

"No," Ruth said, glaring at him.

She scampered back and fell off the bed, hurting her spine on the corner of her bedside table. Her first ever unwarranted injury. She didn't cry out, she didn't want to give him an excuse to come to her. She collected up the remains of her night-light and her duvet and squeezed herself into the small space between her bed and the bedside table. Mam pulled Father from the room. He started to argue again on the landing. Ruth wished she could be just a little bit deaf and blind. She wished Father would go away and never come back. Ruth put her fingers in her ears and hummed "Humpty Dumpty" quietly so she wouldn't hear anything anymore.

5. Ruth

She was still angry at Fletch, even though she didn't see him much. Leanna was a different story, in a way. She saw far too much of her. Max told her one night that Leanna was lonely, and he and Fletch would really appreciate it if Ruth would introduce Leanna to her coven. She laughed at him.

"My coven? Really? Anyway, how can Leanna be lonely?"

She had Fletch and his job was much more high-powered than Max's, surely there were ladies from there that she could befriend. Apparently not. Fletch's job was a hindrance rather than a help. The wives didn't want to spend time with Leanna in case they said anything wrong and it was fed back. This knowledge was beaten into Ruth with blows to her thighs. It was so she couldn't forget it, so she'd have a reminder. It had been weeks since he'd last hit her, she had started to get complacent.

This wasn't the Stepford Wives. They choose to be like that. There were women who worked at Max's company and at Fletch's, but why work when you don't have to, was Ruth's philosophy. She wasn't the only one to think like that either. She and her friends never spent any time or tried to have any friendship with the working women. It was as if that would be insane.

Leanna was not a success with the 'ladies who lunch'. She was difficult to engage and spoke only to say something ironic or sarcastic. Ruth knew what it was all about, but convinced herself she was just paranoid. Leanna was in Ruth's life to watch her, to see what she was up to away from the eyes of Max. All because she had seen how Ruth had behaved around Fletcher on the night of their meal. She found this out on her day of surprises.

She woke up feeling as though something was missing, strange but in no describable way. She went to the bathroom and opened the mirrored cupboard above the sink to get her toothbrush and it hit her as her eyes skittered over an open box of Tampax.

Ruth's period was late and it was usually perfectly on time each month.

She sat down on the edge of the bath, her hands shaking so much that the toothbrush she was holding fell to the floor and bounced behind the toilet. She felt faint and closed her eyes. She waited a moment, wool-gathering as the nausea subsided, then stood up quickly, ignoring the woozy rush of blood to her head. She turned the power shower on full pelt and climbed in before it could even heat properly. She spent a long time under the biting spray thinking things through.

An hour or so later, she walked into a chemist. She had chosen one that was miles away from anyone she knew so that she wouldn't be seen. She had taken a chance before and had been lucky, but was more aware of what she was doing this time, less panicky. She didn't want rumours snaking their way back to Max, be they true or not. That would have destroyed the tenuous peace that was currently reigning over their home. She had already had one negative test, and it might be negative again, or so she hoped. She thought that maybe she was late because of all the stress over Max and Fletcher. She bought herself another pregnancy test, following advice this time from the pharmacist on which was the best, the most accurate. She went to the nearest Waterstone's and bought *The Pregnancy Bible* for herself, and *The Bloke's Guide to Pregnancy*. Even if she was not pregnant, she might be one day and then both would still come in useful. She didn't notice Leanna in the corner of the bookstore. She didn't know Leanna was stalking her and so had no reason to look for the woman in gloomy bookshop shadows.

Once at home, she sat in the bathroom for what felt like a lifetime before deciding to take the pregnancy test. She didn't really want to know the outcome. The drip of the tap in the sink, the only sound in the flat, marked her mounting dread with each plink. Eventually, she was busting to use the toilet anyway and it would have been just a ridiculous waste to urinate and not have bothered.

She poked the end of the stick into the stream as per the instructions. Such a personal procedure for such a personal result. She balanced it on the sink and waited for the answer, for it to tell her where her life was headed. The blue cross; she was pregnant.

"Oh fuck."

Before the news had sunk in, her mobile was ringing. Kylie's 'Can't Get You Out of my Head' made her visibly jump. She answered it after checking the name on the screen, not sure she really wanted to talk to anyone. It was Max; no one important.

"Are you pregnant?"

"Excuse me?" she replied.

"Well, Leanna saw you buying baby books earlier and called to congratulate me, I thought you would have told me first really."

She could hear the anger seeping through his seemingly pleasant tone. She knew instantly that she needed to be careful.

"Leanna? Are you having me followed?"

"Are you? I ought to know."

It dawned on her. The only reason Leanna would call Max before talking to Ruth would be to hurt her. Or maybe them both.

"I *will* tell you first Max, when I'm pregnant. I was just buying them after our chat the other night. You said you would be happy if I did get pregnant. I thought I'd do some preliminary reading."

The lie rolled between her teeth with practiced ease.

"Oh right, sorry, I just thought, you know…"

Her eyes focused on the positive pregnancy test.

"Why has she got your number anyway?" she asked.

"I gave it to her the night we went for that meal, she was really interested in Antigua and said we should meet for coffee to talk about it."

A hesitation told volumes. His lie did not roll off his tongue quite so easily, but Ruth didn't push it, there was no point. It would only end in an argument, and she was fully aware of what would happen after that. Anyway, he wouldn't cheat with Leanna, he

38

wouldn't do that to her, nor to Fletch. She convinced herself once more of his innocence, his perfection.

"Oh, ok, well, I'll see you when you get home. Love you." Even she could hear the sadness in her voice.

She turned off the phone, not wanting his reply. Within a few moments, the home phone started to ring. She ignored it, allowing the answer machine to pick up Max's apologies.

Her head was pounding, she needed to lie down, rest. She took the pregnancy test and wrapped it in toilet roll, put it in the box it came in and then returned it all to the bag from the chemist. She planted the package in a neighbour's rubbish bin, pushing it below the smelly black sacks. Better to be safe than sorry and all that jazz. Denial had always been a constant in her life.

She returned to the flat and lay down on the new sofa in the lounge. It was plump and covered in a chocolate coloured corduroy material, very comfortable and perfect for afternoon snoozing. The new paint and new furniture gave off an aroma of freshness that melted her overwrought mind.

She woke up after only a few minutes' nap and decided to call Leanna. She wouldn't be able to sleep properly until she knew what that woman was up to. She dialled Leanna's mobile number and it rang four times before she answered.

"Oh! Hello Ruth." She sounded as though she had been expecting the call, or maybe Ruth was again, just paranoid.

"Why didn't you say hello in Waterstone's?"

"I only saw you as you left …"

"Saw me well enough to see what I was buying."

Silence.

"Why not be honest Leanna?"

"Did you have an affair with my husband?"

"No, why would I sleep with my boyfriend's best mate?" Ruth was ready for this one. She'd been expecting it for some time, although, Leanna clearly didn't know much about Max, if she did, she would know what a stupid idea cheating on him would be. In

39

fact, if Leanna knew Max well, she wouldn't have even asked the question.

"I know he's had affairs, and normally I turn a blind eye, but at dinner that night, there was something going on between you, I saw it. This is too close to home to ignore."

"I have not slept with Fletcher." If she had any proof, Ruth would be royally screwed.

"Is that the truth?"

"Yes Leanna, the truth, I'm not surprised you don't recognise it for what it is."

"Then I apologise. I've been following you since the night at Fifteen."

This all seemed too easy. Why was she just giving in? She wasn't that type, and this worried Ruth even more.

"So what did you find out from stalking me?" she asked.

"That you and Max are in love with each other and that you have had no contact with my husband. I was about to give up and then I saw you buy those books on pregnancy."

"I don't understand." It was the first candid thing Ruth had said.

"I wanted to make you and Max as unhappy as me and Fletcher. He's having an affair right now; I can smell her every time I come home to the flat after one of our lunches. I don't think I can take it."

The concierge had been right; Ruth was one of many. It was now painfully, blatantly obvious however, that Leanna truly knew nothing about Max. She would've thought Fletch might have told her the horror stories that he had from over the years. He had told Ruth when she had first met Max. But as she had responded, and still believed, Max was different with her. She lied to everyone well, including herself. How awful must it be to live your life like that, like Leanna, she thought. At least with Max, it was all up front; you knew what you were getting. For her, it must be horrendous, having to second guess all the time. She decided to melt. She could see it in others, but never in herself.

"Leanna, I'm sorry. I was trying to make Max jealous to retaliate for him turning our romantic dinner for two into a couples' night out. I'd been dying to go to Fifteen, it really upset me. So I used Fletch, Max didn't notice and unfortunately, you did."

She almost felt bad for Leanna and wanted her to believe she was innocent. Ruth thought that she clearly needed somebody to turn to, and didn't seem to have anybody. It was unimaginable to even consider she was in the same boat. Perhaps if she had, then things would've turned out more favourably for them both.

"That's ok. I'm sure he'll get tired of his latest piece soon enough. So, are you pregnant?"

"No, Max and I were talking about it a couple of nights ago."

"Ok, well I'll leave you in peace, thank you Ruth, and again, I'm sorry."

"No problem."

She returned to the comfort of the sofa to think about what Leanna had said. If she'd needed any more proof, here it was, undeniable confirmation of the tales of the concierge. Some of what Leanna had said was real, a lot of it was a lie and there were some things she had just neglected to mention. Her own affairs, for example. Ruth dozed off again, thinking about Leanna and Max. She dreamt of the two of them kissing each other passionately and laughing at her.

When Max came home from work, he brought Ruth a huge bouquet of flowers and a box of Belgian chocolates from Harrods. He left them on the coffee table next to the sofa. The banging of pots and the strangely overpowering and sickly smell of the flowers woke her up. She opened her eyes and was confronted immediately by the bouquet. They were, in Ruth's opinion, reminiscent of alien plants described in science fiction stories. They quivered and shivered as though at any moment, they might attack. She could hear Max dropping things in the kitchen and swearing. She closed

41

her eyes and groaned quietly. The smell of the flowers was so thick that she would have to move or she would be sick. She wrenched her aching body from the sofa and padded out to Max and the disaster he was creating in her bare feet.

The laminate floor of the kitchen caught her attention first. It was cold and sticky. Her feet seemed to need coaxing to take each step, a pull from the muck on the floor and a push to lay each foot back down The kitchen was a war zone. Pots overflowed on the hob, knocking out the flame, and Max was about to blow the whole place sky high with his futile childish attempts to relight the gas. The worktops were a mess, covered in vegetable peelings and bits of red bleeding meat. Ruth stood in the doorway and watched silently as he put out the fire he had just started in the frying pan. 'How can this catastrophic man ever be a father?' she thought. She ignored the fact that it was unlikely he was the father of the little one growing inside her womb.

Max finally noticed her and turned, grinning like a schoolboy caught stealing apples. Ruth tried to muster a smile but failed. Her nightmares were so vivid and looking at Max and his grin had made them seem even more real. Ruth gasped. He suddenly looked vaguely creepy, like a hallowe'en clown mask. She was scared of him for a split second, and he hadn't even raised his hand.

"Hey, don't look like that. Shall we get a delivery or should we go out to a restaurant tonight?"

"Can't we salvage this?" she asked, wanting to win him over. She walked nervously toward the smoking sink.

"I don't think we can," Max replied. "I think I welded the lamb to the bottom of the frying pan."

She looked more closely at the black mass in the sink, and sure enough, there were some charred lumps solidified onto the non-stick surface of the pan. She couldn't cook either, had never been able to make so much as a dippy egg and soldiers. The fear that her child would starve, or worse, become fat from takeaways spilled into her mind. She felt like crying, it was all so overwhelming.

42

"I think we should go for delivery," she said. "If we go out, we might bump into Leanna and Fletcher again." She flashed a warning look in Max's direction.

Red flush crept from the open neck of his shirt up to his hairline.

"Ruth, it isn't like that. I was just being friendly, that's all."

"Is that why you're blushing?" She thought that he would never cheat on her, but she felt so fractious. She wanted to find a nerve to hit, a line to cross. It was like she wanted an ending to everything.

"Honestly Ruth, I'm serious. I like Leanna but she's just a friend, she's married to my mate for God's sake, I couldn't do that to him."

"Could you do it to me?"

The kitchen was hazy, and the question hung on the smog. She couldn't quite see the look on his face clearly enough. She glared at him as best she could, her eyes stinging from the irritating smoke. He appeared to be imitating a gold fish. She worked her way around the kitchen opening windows and then turned on the extractor to clear the room. Tears were finally streaming down her face, although only those caused by the atmosphere, not those that were pent up inside. She reached the back door and tore it open. The cool air hit her, calming her down as if it were a slap to an hysteric's face. The sweet smell of lavender came up from the end of the courtyard garden on a breeze and her mind eased a little. Enough to make her evaluate the situation and her attitude.

She turned back to assess the damage. Max was still at the cooker, his spatula hanging limp. Her anger deflated and was replaced by sorrow edged with fear. 'Have I just stupidly started something?' she asked herself. She had meant to create a row, but now that she was on the verge of the battle, she panicked. Her paranoia was about her own behaviour and the recent nightmares; it wasn't his fault. It never, ever was though.

43

"Let's get Thai," she said. "And I really don't want you to have anything more to do with Leanna." She needed his security and his love. As much as she was scared of him, she was more scared of losing it all. Every time she gave in, a part of her disappeared into the abyss. It's no wonder there was so little left in the end.

"But…"

"I spoke to her after you called. She says she is trying to make us as miserable as she is with Fletch. And she is succeeding."

"Thai…? I'll order." He walked away to the telephone table, grabbing the menu for the local Thai delivery restaurant from the drawer by the door as he passed. A flash of anger ripped through her as yet again, she realised he was taking over, making her choices. She was clearly going to get what she was given.

6. Max

I love you, Ruth. Just so you know. I never meant to do what I did.
I want to make it up to you, but you're already punishing me.
Squeeze my hand, please. I'll read today, how would that be? I
know you like this one, it's *Catch 22*. The bit where he dreams
about the fish. You used to always laugh when you read that bit. It
used to annoy me, you giggling away on the sofa while you read. I
felt excluded and unimportant. Still, I'll try. I'll give anything a go.

Why aren't you laughing? You know, it's really hard to keep
trying when there's no response. I think that was what went wrong
in the first place. You never responded to me. Never loved me in
the way I loved you. Everyone said you were a gold digger when I
first met you. They told me to walk away. But I thought you were
different. I mean, I know you were living with someone else when
we met, but that was different, he treated you badly, you told me. I
never treated you like he did. I know I didn't. I mean we had fights
and stuff, but you've never cheated on me. Still though, sometimes I
wonder, do you really love me in the way I love you? It hurts me to
ask that, and it hurts more that you can't answer. My guess is, it's a
little of both. I think you might have softened a bit over the years,
but maybe not enough. I think, that when you wake up, we'll need
to talk this stuff through. Get it straight in our heads. Make sure
we're both in for the long run for the same reasons. I'll change. I
really will.

Man, why am I saying this? It's not true, I know it isn't. I
guess just being sat here and talking into thin air hoping you can
hear me is driving me insane and giving me thoughts that just aren't
real. Ignore me. Ignore all I've said. Except for the bit about me
changing. That's going to happen. They don't know where the
bruises came from, and I said I didn't either. They made me feel
sick. I can't believe what I've done to you.

Do you remember that day when I came back from Antigua
and you'd been to a health farm? The house and the garden was in

45

such a state, I sacked the cleaning company we'd used. I think they must have thrown a wild party when we were away, but all they said to me was, "I'm sorry Mr. Parker, the house was in a terrible state when we got there, we did the best we could."

I was so angry with them for upsetting you. I wish you could have come with me. Antigua was fantastic, but nothing without you. You must have got pregnant in that week I came back, God it was fun.

You're still being classed as critical, but the doctor said not to give up yet. He offered me counselling. But I just can't leave you until you can breathe on your own. He said that I should talk to you as much as I can. He said that you might be able to hear me. Some people in your situation can. They come round and remember snippets of conversations that went on while they lay there. Trapped.

He said not to lose hope. That's all they keep saying. Every two minutes someone else comes in here with another needle or chart or thermometer. They test you over and over again as if they're just going to keep trying until you pass their exam. Do you know, I can't remember you ever telling me anything about your life before me? Did you take exams at school? College? University? Did you do any of those things? What did you want to be when you grew up? What do you want to be now? I know nothing about you really. I think you know everything about me.

This room is awful. They've put you on a ward. A special ward for special people. Two have already died this morning and it's only eleven. The only thing that separates me and you from the people either side is a flimsy curtain. I can hear everyone around me whispering wishes to the people they visit. It's very quiet in here. Except for when someone starts crying. Usually that means someone they love has died. I hope that doesn't happen to us.

"Hi."

"Hello Mr. Parker."

"Please call me Max, Nurse…?"

46

"It's Sally, I'm just going to check Ruth's blood pressure, ok? Won't take a moment."

"Ok."

"How're you holding up?"

"Ok, I guess."

"Once we're sure she can breathe by herself, we'll move her out of the intensive care unit, put you both somewhere more comfortable."

"Do you think that will happen?"

"Possibly. There, all done. Just buzz if you need anything."

I don't like the way she looked at me. It's like they all know. It's like you've been talking when I'm not around, and I've only been taking bathroom breaks.

Five days I've sat here with you. Five days. We should be at home, just married, in the first flush of commitment, sorting our stuff out for the move, preparing for the baby. There's only six weeks left now you know. Just six weeks. We're supposed to be moving into our new place in about three weeks. The decorators are still booked to go in next week. I haven't cancelled them. I never saw your ideas, so I thought I'd let them get on with it, with the instructions you left and then I could surprise myself. It won't be right though. Not unless you're there with me.

I feel so useless. I can't do anything to make you well. I wish I was a doctor. I should have done medicine at university instead of business. I would have known all that was going on if I'd done that. I'd be able to interpret your charts back into English and know how well you're doing. I'd know what drugs you needed. I'd know how much. I could be the one making you *you* again. I could make amends for you being here in the first place. I thought about going home and looking stuff up on the internet. But then I realised if I typed "car accident" and "coma" into Google I'd see all sorts of things that I really would never want to see.

I must cheer up you know. This is hard enough as it is without me being some morbid pathetic loser as well. I just want something positive to happen. It's not too much to ask. Actually, what I really want, is to turn back the clock to that night we went to Fifteen. I want us to not go to Fifteen and for everything else, except your pregnancy of course, to be different. If I could do that, we wouldn't be here now. I know that. Don't worry, I don't blame you for any of this. I blame me. And the taxi driver who wrecked our wedding day.

The doctor's started his rounds again. I can hear him telling people in whispers what they need him to shout. They talk so much gobbldegook though. I only get half of what he says to me. I'm bright, but no, it's like ringing the Inland Revenue. Their main aim in life is to blind you with science so that you don't know what the hell is going on and therefore they don't have to really tell you anything. He'll be with us soon. More poking and prodding. More jargon. This really is the worst experience of my life.

"Good Morning Mr. Parker, now let me have a look here...ah yes...Right, I think we shall try and remove the tube today that breathes for Ruth. She has made fantastic progress in the last twenty-four hours, and hopefully, she'll be able to breathe on her own now."

"And what if she can't?"

"Then we'll re-insert the tube and discuss the options."

Dear God I hope you can breathe on your own. Shit, he's coming back.

"Are you doing it now?"

"No time like the present. Right, Nurse? Gently does it, that's it. Come on Ruth, there's a good girl."

Breathe Ruth, breathe, please breathe.

"Wonderful. Nurse, frequent obs and oxygen. Mr. Parker, this is fantastic progress. I'll be back again later to see how she's doing. There is hope yet."

You did it, oh thank God you did it. Now, just keep on breathing. You can wake up properly another day if you want. For

48

today, I'll just be happy with breathing. I knew something good would have to happen eventually.

7. Ruth

She ignored her impending child, continued with her daily life by suppressing the niggling baby thoughts to the back of her mind. She realised eventually, that she would need to make a doctor's appointment. She'd convinced herself in the interim period between tests one and two, and then two and now, that over the counter pregnancy tests were never entirely accurate, so she should therefore get a professional opinion. She thought that she probably wasn't even pregnant. She would also like to have the chance to abort before Max unknowingly did it for her. It would be a very difficult decision, perhaps the hardest one of her life, but she just was not sure that it would be right to bring a baby into the relationship. Perhaps her suppressed childhood memories were worming their way back into her conscious mind as early as then, whether she knew it or not. Her subconscious was warning her to understand the hesitation, the worry, of subjecting another child to those experiences. She ignored it as much as she ignored the potential pregnancy.

Max came home from work in a dreadful mood. He had been struggling with the new office layout. She told him that she hadn't been feeling quite herself lately and so would be going to see the doctor in the morning. His mood shifted in an instant. He became like an over-excited puppy, bouncing around the flat with ideas for names, birthing techniques and plans for a new home. She viciously cut him down, bringing him back to normality.

"It might just be a bad case of thrush."

Perhaps she shouldn't have said anything to him. The trouble was, if she kept secrets from Max, he would be remarkably angry when they eventually came out. He was already pretty hacked off after the last episode, and if someone saw her as she came out of the doctor's surgery, all hell would break out. It just wasn't worth it. She could always lie and say she was not pregnant once she'd had the appointment, but to lie about going, that would be too difficult to get out of if she was caught.

He instantly became sulky and sat watching the television in silence. She could feel the anger simmering in him all evening. He didn't go to bed until after she had fallen asleep. She felt terrible, but didn't want him to get too excited, to make decisions for her regarding the child. She hadn't decided if she would keep the baby yet. What if she told him and then, it turned out that she wasn't pregnant, or even worse, she decided that she wanted an abortion? It would be better that she kept it to herself for a while longer. Until she knew for certain, and decided what would be best on her own.

She left the doctor's surgery, her handbag stuffed to bursting point with leaflets on antenatal classes, health advice for pregnant women and birthing options. Her mind was reeling. She walked to the local park, the same one with the toilets of falsehood. She sat on a bench in the soul-warming sunshine and closed my eyes. She could clearly hear children laughing and shouting in the play area. 'I'm going to have one of those,' she thought and almost threw up. She had always assumed that when she first became pregnant, she'd be excited and happy, but she just felt very sad. She should have realised, she should have got herself some help. She could've said something to the doctor when she had asked about Ruth's partner, but some things are far too difficult to voice. She drove home with the radio turned off: silence allowed her to think a little more freely. Silence allowed solitude. It just could not be Fletcher's, and that was final. On the way back, she stopped to pick up some wrapping paper covered in baby motifs. She arrived home, wrapped up the book on pregnancy for men and left it on the coffee table. A coffee table book that showed not sophistication, but real life, a piece of yellow wrapped up tack that actually seemed to accentuate the room. It was too cheerful, too bright, but that was just due to her frozen brain. In reality, it was just perfect for its job.

She was waiting for Max in nervous silence when he came in, unsure of how to proceed. She knew he wanted a baby. He

51

always seemed to light up when the idea was mentioned. Even so, what if when the dream became a reality, he felt differently? There was a half-drunk cold cup of coffee next to the yellow obscenity on the table. She looked up at his eager face, wondering what had got him so excited. She hadn't told anybody yet, she had nobody to tell, so he couldn't know. It took her hours to decide to keep it. It just could not be Fletcher's. It couldn't.

"I've got something to tell you," they said in perfect unison.

"Will you marry me?" Max asked. He knelt in front of her. He grinned at her manically, expectantly. The same grin he'd had when she found him wrecking the kitchen. She was too shocked to reply straight away, she hadn't anticipated this happening.

"Will you?"

He produced a velvet box from his pocket and opened it. Inside was a beautiful platinum diamond solitaire engagement ring. She took the ring from the box, revelled in the expense of it, and marvelled at how little he know about her. If he'd known her at all, there would've been rubies and diamonds. Something more colourful, but less ostentatious. Always, the money got her. Money wasn't everything, there were things that just weren't worth material gain. She should've learnt that as a child, but she could be slow in learning from the past and history kept repeating for her. It had always been the same. Gifts just never say sorry properly. The only thing that said sorry properly was when the event never happened again. She couldn't marry him hiding a lie, she shouldn't marry him at all really. He wasn't safe, he wouldn't be stable. What if he hurt their baby? Her brain whirred as she tried to examine the pros and cons of his proposal in seconds that might have tumbled into hours were she not practiced.

"Yes," she replied.

He took the ring from her and slid it gently onto her finger. They both started to cry, hugging each other tightly, snuffling in each other's comfort and joy. They broke apart at last, she was feeling silly, but so relieved. This was, to her, a sure sign Max had changed. They had been together for two and a half years, and he had never even mentioned marriage before. If he wasn't the father, she thought he'd stand by her once they were married. Maybe the baby wouldn't look like Fletch. Maybe they would never know. That was too wishful. If it was Fletch's, then it would have his colouring. There would be no denying it then, that was for sure. Ruth however, had lost another little part of her will to their relationship and could now convince herself of anything to make life bearable.

She reached across to the table and picked up the present.

"It's nothing to the ring, but it's something."

He opened it and looked at the title, bewildered for a fleeting moment. The perplexity drifted from his face like a dead leaf falling from the bough of a tree.

"Oh my God. Oh. My. God."

She stared at him waiting for him to say more. She screamed as he jumped up, laughing and crying. He reached down and lifted her into his arms. She was shivering with fear. Her emotions flipped within milliseconds. It would be years of new nice non-violent Max before she stopped that reaction to his every sudden movement.

"Oh my God Ruth. How amazing; oh my God. I love you!"

She laughed along with him, but it was faked. She cried too, but because she was lying; she was feeling guilty and she was scared, terrified even.

"I've got to ring my Mum and tell her, she's going to be ecstatic."

She slumped on the sofa while he was on the phone. Ruth had no one to tell. Everyone had gone from my life, left her in one way or another. She felt overwhelmed by a sadness that never went away, mourning her losses for the millionth billionth time. Her heart was blackened by multitudes grief. Max came back and flopped down next to her.

"Who do you want to call?" he asked.

53

"Who do I have to call?"

He knew that she had nobody. Not even a friend of her own. Another knife twist, another shackle chained. She'd never actually told him anything about her past. Nothing. But she had told him when they had met that she had nobody. She thought that perhaps that was one of the reasons he had liked her so much. No baggage.

"Sorry Ruth, I forgot." He appeared truly remorseful and she didn't want to ruin the evening, so she bit back and just smiled. What it took her to smile when she was crumbling inside. She had no family, no friends, nothing. Her family, as far as she knew, were all dead in one way or another. Her friends were all Max's, she had nobody, and still she didn't see the problem.

"Let's go out and celebrate, I'll call around to everyone, yeah?"

"No," she said. "Let's stay in tonight and just celebrate together."

She'd agreed to marry a man knowing that she might not be carrying his child. She didn't even know if she honestly loved Max. She wasn't sure how love felt. She didn't think she had ever been in love. 'I am in love. I'm just scared,' she decided. He had changed, she needed to hang onto that knowledge and let it enable her to continue to love him unconditionally. 'We all make mistakes. I do love him.' She had made her decision. All she could do now was marry him and hope he was the father. Max left her alone to buy a bottle low alcohol wine, an oxymoron as far as she was concerned. She ordered in yet another takeaway. She almost told the takeaway manager that she was pregnant, just so she could tell someone herself, but sanity prevailed and she stuck to their usual weather chat prior to placing her order. They spent time alone, looking at the pamphlets from the doctor and the books she had bought. They curled up to watch the television.

"How long did you know about being pregnant?"

She had been hoping that he wouldn't ask.

"I was only sure today."

"But when did you first think you might be?"

"The day you thought I might be, but I took a test and it was negative."

"Why didn't you tell me?"

She averted her eyes, staring at the scattered takeaway boxes, empty aside from some residual crud, looking for an answer.

"Because I didn't think I was, there was no point getting your hopes up, was there?"

"I thought we had an open relationship."

In more ways than one.

"We do Max, and I didn't lie, I told you I wasn't pregnant, because that was the truth at the time, and now I've found out differently, I've told you."

She was on high alert, this would be a catalyst if ever she had seen one. If she was not careful, he could kill her for this, for keeping a secret. Secrets weren't allowed, although she did have some. Her secrets helped to keep her sane.

He turned away to watch the television. His arm around her stiffened, and his face was set as though he was trying to hold back something he wanted to say. She didn't want to ask, she didn't want to know. She was pregnant and they were going to get married. She admired her ring watching it glint in the soft light from the floor lamps. She saw Max's eyes shift towards her hand. He was fighting his temper, it was like she could watch him doing it, as though there were two physical beings at war with one another. *Celebrity Death Match* round one; Max Parker versus Max Parker's Temper! DING DING!

"Come on, there's still time to go out," she said, hoping to placate him.

"Let's invite everybody here," he replied.

"Ok, I need a shower and to get changed, can you call round?" she agreed just to placate him.

Max got the phone and his address book. She headed into the bathroom. She wanted him to be happy, to be calm and relaxed.

55

She spent as long as she could pampering and pruning herself, and when she came out, Max was in the bedroom, changing out of his work suit into casuals. She put on a Prada ensemble that she knew he particularly liked. He'd bought it for her as a sorry gift. They didn't talk to each other.

She returned to the living room to await the guests; Max had tidied up and put *his* CDs out for *his* people to choose *his* music. Oasis, Blur, nineties rejects just like them. She could hear Max moving around in the bathroom. The toilet flushed, water ran into the sink. It impressed her that they could be so close and yet the distance between them seemed so great. She perched on the arm of the sofa, distantly admiring the warm tones she had used in decorating the room. Max went into the kitchen and she could hear the chink of glass as he set up the numerous bottles of alcohol on the counter. He returned to the living room and looked down at her, she watched him from the corner of her eye, not yet ready to meet his gaze.

"I love you Ruth," he said.

"I know you do Max, I love you too," she replied.

Before he could say any more, the doorbell rang. She stood up and left to answer it without looking at him, avoiding him like she would avoid Medusa were they in the same room. She put on her imitation smile and greeted the first guests, as any good hostess should. She showed them into the lounge and Max, buoyant once again, saw to their drinks. The doorbell rang again. She excused herself politely and braced herself to be the gracious hostess for a second time.

"Fletcher, Leanna, how good to see you." She could've had a career as an actress.

Fletcher smirked, kissed her cheek and marched past her into the lounge to greet Max. Leanna smiled more honestly and asked, "So, what are we celebrating?"

"You'll find out soon enough," Ruth replied.

56

Her face changed at lightning speed and she strutted through on her sky high stilettoes to join the others. Ruth continued to greet guests as they arrived until finally, Max shouted above the noise to say they had an announcement. Everyone went quiet and turned to look at the two of them. Max pinned Ruth to his side, there was no escape now, as if there ever had been.

"Ruth and I are getting married."

A roar of male approval leapt to her ears, the ladies clapped politely.

"And furthermore, we are expecting our first child."

His hand patted her stomach like it was a good dog. 'What is it with men and their insistence on patting the pregnant stomach, even when there's no bump? Why do they do that?' she thought behind her sparkling smile. It made her feel like she was his toy, which in truth, she was. Everyone cheered this time. She winced through the smile that had top be plastered onto her face until her cheeks ached, and then she smiled some more. She accepted the individual congratulations graciously as they came from Max's friends and colleagues, their girlfriends and wives. She sipped her low alcohol sparkling wine and wished it were vodka with a twist of lime. Max avoided her and they separately mingled amongst his people. She was affable enough, so as not to alienate, but she wished continuously that all these people would leave. His people.

The party ended around one in the morning. Ruth was exhausted but once everyone had gone, she wanted them back again. She didn't want to be alone with Max. She went to the bathroom to get ready for bed, passing him silently in the hallway. Leanna was in there, the door open. She looked unusually rumpled and her red lipstick was smudged over her upper lip. Ruth stared at her as she straightened her clothes, a second or two passed before she noticed Ruth in the doorway.

"Ruth, you made me jump."

She looked like a rabbit caught in the headlights.

"Are you ok?" Ruth asked.

57

"Fine, yes, just tidying myself up. Fletch and I have been making another go of it, and you know how it is, make-up sex and all that, we just can't keep our hands off each other."

"I thought Fletch left ten minutes ago." As she spoke, the doorbell rang again. Max answered it and the two women listened to Fletch's raucous voice as it floated down the hallway to them.

"He went to get the car while I sorted out my face."

"Oh."

Leanna looked at Ruth with what might be considered sympathy. She made one more check in the mirror, and then left, brushing against Ruth in the doorway. Ruth went into the bathroom at last and closed the door behind her. The lip. It was still smudged. Fletch wasn't here. Max was in the hallway. She didn't want to believe what her eyes were telling her. She couldn't. Max wasn't that kind of man. She had not got engaged to a replica of Father. She knew better than that. She had always avoided that kind of man. She was sure she had. Was she really that naïve? She brushed her teeth and then exfoliated and moisturised on autopilot before going into the bedroom. She could hear Max in the living room, tidying. It wound her up to the point of screaming that he could never leave it until the morning. She was sleep before he came in.

How wrong she was. Every man had been like her Father. She had never avoided his presence. Every man she had ever been involved with had all been cheaters, most of them beaters too. Max was most certainly one of those doubled prizes.

8. Little Ruth

Father woke up very late the next day. Mam was in the kitchen with Ruth, trying to coax her to eat a Farley's Rusk with a glass of milk when Father came down. He kissed Mam on the cheek and she winced as his skin brushed hers.

"What happened to your eye?" Father asked, some concern in his voice.

"You did," Mam muttered.

And then some. The physical evidence was always sparse, both for her and for Ruth. It was the other injuries. The memories that never let up. The bruises hidden under clothes. The breaks that healed themselves. For Ruth, it had always been the memories that were the worst, the evidence in her brain that tortured her constantly.

Her Father came to where Ruth sat at the table and said, "Good Morning sweetheart, Daddy's missed you."

He bent to kiss her forehead, and Ruth flinched away from him. She started to cry; rich, heartbreaking sobs shook through her body. She climbed off her chair and scrambled under the table. Father stared at her with large eyes, he did not get angry.

"Why's she acting like that?" he asked Mam.

"Because of you."

"What did I do?" His voice bristled with confusion and anger, as though he was on the defence, as though he had not been on the attack.

"You scared the living daylights out of her last night when you came home, and you broke her night-light. It's all she can talk about."

"I don't remember that, you're lying woman."

"I'm not Rick. *You* were drunk. *You* frightened her."

Father poked his head under the table, the little girl scooted away on her bottom, propelling herself backwards with her hands and not taking her eyes from him. She watched him as intently as he watched her. Ruth tried to think to him her anger and fear because

59

she was crying too hard to speak. After a moment that seemed like ages, he stood up and she could only see his legs.

"What have I done?" he asked, recognition lacing every word.

"You have to sort yourself out, we can't go on like this, she won't eat again."

"I'll make more of an effort this time, I will, I promise."

He walked over to Mam. Ruth peeked out from under the table and watched him hug her. Oh how she wished that her Mam had more strength. She had strength, a lot of strength. She just used it to try to change him instead of to try to leave him.

"Can you take Ruth swimming or something? Take her out for most of the day? I want to do something special," he said, handing Mam a bunch of notes, before going back upstairs. The reds and purples told Ruth it was a lot of money. The look on Mam's face made it clear it was a huge amount. Money solves nothing. It is not an apology.

Mam helped Ruth out from under the table and tried to get her to eat again. She still refused, but she did sit at the table, if only so that she could watch for his return. It wasn't long before he came back dressed and putting his coat on. He kissed Mam goodbye and smiled at Ruth. He took a step towards her and she shrank away, so he waved goodbye from the sink.

Ruth didn't want to go swimming; she was too tired from her lack of sleep the night before, so Mam took her for a drive through the country. They stopped at a field full of cows and one tried to eat Ruth's red sandal through the gape in the big gate. The cow made her giggle, Mam cried a little bit at that. Ruth asked her why and her Mam said it was because she had made such a beautiful sound and that she didn't get to hear beautiful sounds very often.

Mam took her for tea and ice cream in a little café. Ruth ate her ice cream in silence watching the cars go by through the window. The ice cream was nice and she hadn't eaten for a few days, so she felt a little perkier when she'd finished it. Mam said she was very proud of her.

They took the long route home because Mam let Ruth choose the way. Finally, they pulled into their road and she could see her Father's hired car parked outside the house. Balloons had been tied to the gate and the front door. Mam told her to wait in the car while she checked Father was ready. Ruth felt nervous as Mam went to the front door and let herself in. Fear of what might be waiting for her inside the house when she went in gnawed at her spine. But Mam returned smiling broadly. Ruth looked into her eyes when she came to the car but could see nothing scary hiding in them and so went with Mam into the house. She really hated surprises, and she always would, but Mam seemed to think things were alright.

Mam took her into the kitchen where a party table for three had been set up. The tablecloth was bright and cheerful; the napkins were red to match the horses on the tablecloth. There were paper plates at the settings with plastic knives and forks. Coned paper hats with party pictures on them sat on the plates. Streamers in red, blue and green decorated the chairs. Mam led her to her chair and sat her down. On the paper plate was a picture of a clown face. Mam put the hat on Ruth's head; the elastic strap ran behind her ears and under her chin, cutting into her flesh, but she wouldn't say anything. Mam put on a hat too and sat down next to Ruth.

She was confused, she didn't know what was going on. She never went to parties. Friends could be hard to come by when they could never come and play at your house. It wasn't Christmas, and Ruth didn't think it was anyone's birthday, so she didn't know why there was a party. Before she could ask Mam, her Father came in carrying three badly wrapped presents. He placed them in the centre of the table.

"And I cooked, Ruth," he said.

Ruth watched dubiously as he opened the oven door and smoke came out in foggy clouds. Her Father laughed as he waved it away and proceeded to burn himself, again and again, as he tried to

61

remove the blackened pot from the oven. She started to smile a little when he burnt himself for the fourth time. He eventually salvaged the wreck of his cooking from the oven and brought it to the table where he set it between himself and Mam.

"It's cheese-potato pie, Mummy told me it's your new favourite. I can scrape off the black bits."

Ruth didn't want to say anything that might make him angry again, so she slipped from her chair and went to Mam's side. She pulled Mam close to her and whispered in her ear, so quietly that the words were almost lost to the breeze.

"What is it? Is it because I burnt it?" Father asked.

His face was the dictionary definition of worry and pain, that frightened the little girl even more. If he got upset, or was scared, or worried, or any strong emotion really, it could lead straight to the pounding of fists.

"She doesn't want to upset you, but she's frightened of the clown on her plate, she hates clowns."

"She's daft," Father said. Ruth didn't like the tone of his voice and she started to shake.

"Let me get her another plate," Mam sounded worried, and Ruth could understand why.

"No, I'll get it," he sighed, "Does she have a favourite?"

"Her Starbright one," Mam replied.

Father went to the cupboard and got her special plate and swapped it for the evil clown.

"I got paper especially so there'd be no washing up," he grumbled, but good naturedly this time.

"I know, but one plate won't matter."

He dumped a dollop of the burnt potato onto Starbright's face.

The dinner went well. Ruth and Mam chatted to Father and he listened intently. He told jokes that made them all laugh, not rude ones, but some were close. He asked Ruth if she liked her tea, and although it was horrible, she told him it was lovely. She thought

62

secretly that she'd never like cheese-potato pie ever again. Finally, when all was finished (they'd even had special Neopolitan ice cream for dessert), Father made a speech.

"I wanted to tell you that I'm really sorry that I frightened you both last night and that I hurt Mummy. I promise it will never happen again."

Ruth sat in unconvinced silence watching him but trying her best to believe what he said.

"I bought you both a present or two today, partly to say sorry, but also because I want you to look at these things and know I mean that I will never do anything like that again." *Bloody presents. Always bloody presents.*

He handed Ruth the second biggest present. She looked at Mam for affirmation that it would be ok to open it. Mam smiled at her and so she started to peel back the paper. Inside was a box with a picture of a Princess on the front. Ruth looked at Father, confused by why there would be a Princess in a box.

"It's a new night-light. A Rapunzel one," he said.

Ruth started to cry, she was sad at the loss of the Old Woman in the Shoe, but she was so happy to have a real Princess to light her room at night. Father looked startled and turned to her Mam. Even then, he had no idea of who she was or how he should behave around her. If only he'd asked why she was crying, she might've been able to tell him. She might not, because he scared her inside and out again, but she might.

"Are you crying because you're happy?" Mam said.

Ruth didn't really know all the words she would need to explain her complicated feelings, so she just nodded, because obviously, from the tone of Mam's voice, crying with happiness was alright. Father laughed and picked her up in a tight hug. He kissed her cheek and sat her on his knee while he passed the smallest present to Mam.

Mam opened her gift and gasped.

"It's beautiful!"

Father had given her a bracelet. It was gold and had some small sparkly bits in it. Ruth thought it was very pretty. She started to believe her Father's words. She understood that the bracelet must have cost a lot of money, and that for him to have spent so much, he must've been really very sorry indeed.

Next, Father gave Ruth the biggest present. She opened it carefully, still sitting on his knee. He wouldn't let her have it on her lap because he said it was too heavy, so she awkwardly reached over the table to take off the paper. He had bought her a pair of Fisher-Price roller skates, the kind that went over your shoes and could be set at different levels to make them easier or harder to use. They were blue, red and yellow. They looked shiny and grown-up in the picture on the box. She looked up at Father and this time, she kissed his bristly cheek. He must really mean what he says, she thought.

"Can I try them today?" she asked.

"Of course you can." said Father.

Mam and Father cleaned up the debris from the meal together, laughing and kissing each other. Ruth watched and was fairly certain that he really was going to be nice now. Then, they went to the concrete car park for the allotments over the road and Father helped Ruth put on her new skates. She stumbled around the car park on the easy level, scraping her knees every now and again. Mam and Father watched, their arms linked around each other's waists while they gave her encouragement and told her how proud they were of her and took it in turns to pick her up when she fell.

After half an hour or so, they all went indoors because it was getting dark. Mam made hot chocolate for them all and they sat on the sofa to watch *Casualty*. Ruth sat in between her two parents, relishing the comfort and their laughter. She felt happy in the presence of Father for the first time in many months. Finally she dozed off to sleep and knew nothing more until she awoke in her own bed the next morning with her new night-light on the top of the chest of drawers next to her.

For the final few days that Father was at home, she had a wonderful time. He took her to try her roller skates every day and he was kind and helpful at home. Most of all, he didn't drink any alcohol, or at least, not as far as Ruth could tell. She kept sniffing him to make sure. This impressed upon her his determination to change more than anything else. There were lots of cuddles and kisses in the house. Mam even stopped flinching whenever Father came near. To Ruth, home was perfect and delicious. She ate with Mam and Father at every mealtime. She stopped hiding in her room for hours at an end, no longer sitting in the bottom of her wardrobe with her teddy in her arms.

On his last day, Father took lots of photos of Ruth and Mam. He had a very posh new Olympus camera, which Ruth and Mam had never seen before. Father said he had bought it in Duty Free; Mam looked confused. Ruth also felt rather mystified as she had never heard of a place by that name. She thought it must be the name of that hot place where Father worked. She wasn't allowed to touch the camera, but Father did show her how it worked and how he could turn the lens a bit and take close-ups of Mam's face without moving nearer to her. Ruth thought it was amazing and asked Father to bring one home for her next time he came. Father laughed and said he'd see what he could do, but really, cameras were grown-up toys.

In the afternoon, it was time to say goodbye, Ruth cried, so did Mam. Father looked sad as he kissed them goodbye, but he didn't cry. Ruth sat on the wall that separated the front garden from the pavement and listened to Mam and Father as they said their goodbyes in the street.

"Why do you have to go so soon? What happened to your second week of leave?" Mam asked.

"I've only got one week this time, I thought I'd told you that?" Father replied.

"I don't remember, I'm sorry, I wish you could stay longer, it's been so nice this time, you've changed and I love it," Mam said.

"I'll be home again soon, and next time it'll be just as great, I promise."

Father kissed Mam on the nose and then came across to where Ruth sat, he picked her up and she put her arms around his neck, feeling his new beard brush against her arm made her shiver.

"Now, you look after Mummy won't you? Make her laugh so she's not sad while I'm gone."

"I will," Ruth replied, "but why can't you work in and Office like other Daddies? I don't like Duty Free."

Father laughed so hard, he shook and Ruth bounced on his hip. "Just like that," he said.

Father took Ruth over to Mam, kissed her cheek, kissed Mam's lips and then got in the car and drove away. How many goodbyes were necessary in this world?

9. Max

We went to Fifteen, didn't we? Of course we did, I've talked about it to you loads already, but I just can't get that night out of my head. You were so excited. I know that having Leanna and Fletch there ruined your evening a bit, and me and Fletch getting wasted ruined it a lot more, but it was a good night. I couldn't help them being there. Fletch got me the reservation and one for himself. It was a favour owed to him by one of his clients. I just didn't expect that to annoy you. I was sorry, honestly Ruth. I know I say sorry a lot, but after this, I won't ever have to say sorry again. Everything will be different. I hope you don't leave me. I hope you can hear me. It's all going to be alright. You, me and the baby, and no more stuff going on. No more fights.

You went mental for a week after that, blitzing the flat and stuff. I thought you were pregnant even then, but you didn't think so. Preening the house, throwing up, all the signs were there. I was just so angry that you weren't telling me, that you were keeping it all to yourself. Everyday, I wanted to say something to you, and in the end, I figured you were just being malicious. That's why I asked you to marry me. I figured that you'd tell me then, once I'd done that. I didn't realise you were going to tell me that day anyway.

I'm going to sing for you now. I know you love the sound of my off-key warbling.

Slip inside the eye of your mind
Don't you know you might find
A better place to play
You said that you'd never been
All the things that you've seen
Slowly fade away

That's not really funny, is it? Well, I have a little stereo here, just for you, and a collection of your favourite albums. The doctor

67

said it was a good idea, do you agree? Why don't you answer me? Ha ha ha. Let's try Queen's *Greatest Hits*, I remember you telling me when we first met that it was your ultimate…

"Leanna, what are you doing here?"

"She's dead Max, leave her, I still love you."

"She's not dead yet, and I love *her*. I should've ended it when she found out, I was wrong not to, and we both know that."

"But Max…"

"Go back to Fletch, if he'll still have you."

"I don't want him I want you."

"I'll call security Leanna, I'm warning you."

"But I thought we were building something together."

I know I promised I'd never hit you again, but that doesn't mean I won't hit anyone. Sometimes my temper just gets away from me, but that's Leanna gone now. I don't think she'll be back. If she does, then I'll do things properly, I won't get angry, I'll ask them to get security in and make her leave. I won't do it again.

Oh bugger. I'm sorry, I truly am. Did you know? Is that what brought all this on? I tried to hide it from you, it was just sex, you wouldn't do anything, you didn't want to hurt the baby. I guess it just suited me at the time. That sounds so nasty, but I didn't mean it to be that way. I didn't mean it to happen. I felt as though you didn't love me. As though I was just some pawn in your game. That's why we kept fighting. In a way, it was all your own fault. Do you know, in all the time we've been together, you have never said 'I love you' to me. Never. I've never heard those words from your lips. Leanna did, she told me she loved me all the time. I told you it started that night at the party. But by then, it had been going on for ages.

It started after that meal. The day after. I might as well tell you the whole truth now, while you can't leave me or argue back, not that you'd do either, would you? That's why I love you so much. She rang me and asked if I was free at lunch. She'd picked up some brochures on Antigua but couldn't find the right hotel. I

68

said yes. I picked her up from hers and we drove out into the country. We had a pub lunch. A nice old fashioned ploughman's. See that's what got me to start off with. None of that fancy stuff for her, I could never have taken you out to a place like that.

We went for a walk after lunch, into some woods. We talked about so much, all my worries about you and whether you loved me or not and all her stuff about Fletch cheating. I don't know if any of it was true now. We ended up in a clearing in the middle of nowhere. We sat down and she cried, I put my arm around her to comfort her and the next thing I knew, we were kissing.

God Ruth, I am so sorry, I didn't want you to find out. I told you about the party, told you it was a one night thing. Did you know? You caught us later, but did you know how much had been going on? Did you know for how long? When you caught us, I think I said that was the last time, but in truth, I'm no longer sure how many times you almost caught us again after that. I kept telling myself you weren't bright enough to figure out what was going on. So, did you? That's the million dollar question that might give me an answer. I need a break, I need to clear my head. I promise she's left now, I'm not going after her. I'm just going to the canteen for a cup of tea. I'll be right back.

10. Ruth

Ruth woke up late and Max was still lying beside her. She could tell he was awake. He was silent, lying on his side with his back to her, stiff as a corpse. She reciprocated. She didn't want to move in case it started a row. The air in the room was stale and stuffy, like the last hour before a thunderstorm. He clearly had something to say, if not, then he would have gone to work as normal. The time on the DVD player read ten in the morning, so he should definitely have been at work. He sighed, but did not speak. She was sure he knew she was awake. She lay perfectly still, a deer caught in the headlights of impending doom.

Someone had to make the first move and she would be damned if it was going to be her. She was not quite that stupid. The green digital counter, luminous in the half-light of the room, ticked over each minute. She watched it, unable to go back to sleep, determined not to stay awake. The battle of wills continued. At eleven oh eight, Max sighed again and got out of bed, he left the room stomping and banged the door into the wall as he went past. She heard him in the bathroom. She got up a few minutes after he had and went into the kitchen to make coffee. She used the Tefal so that it would be fresh and good. As far as she knew, or at least, thought she knew, she was not in the wrong here. She had given him his party; she had behaved impeccably. She had accepted his proposal, and she would be having a child for him. For herself. She would have the child for herself and no one else.

She sat in the Breakfast Nook staring out at the back garden, waiting for the coffee to percolate. She was completely delusional in many ways. She wanted perfection, but the mistakes... Max walked into the kitchen. Enough coffee had dripped through for one cup. Just. He poured it for himself and sat down directly in Ruth's sightline.

"So," he said.

70

"So what?" Perhaps she was gunning for a fight too. Or perhaps her hormones were playing havoc with her common sense, turning her into a loose canon, a crazy cat lady.

He pursed his lips and looked down into his coffee. She felt like she had done something terrible, but she didn't know what. He had said he would change, but the current atmosphere made her wonder. She felt as though he would wait, sighing and pursing, until she worked it out, or eternity ended, whichever came first. Unless he knew about Fletch, she thought, but Fletch would never have told. The tension was destroying her. Her stomach was churning, her head was pounding and she had only been awake for an hour and a half. She stared belligerently at his crown, trying to hide her smile as she realised she could see the beginnings of hair loss. He sighed again.

"I can't take this anymore," she said. "What the fuck have I done wrong?"

He flinched at her words. She never swore in front of him, he hated women swearing, said it was uncouth. He didn't even really swear himself. He still didn't look up from his coffee however, but his right hand twitched twice, as if it was itching to whip out across the table and slap her puffy, pregnant woman's face. His breath made miniature waves on the surface of the coffee.

"You've done nothing wrong," he said.

That was a first! She should've recorded that one, recorded it to memory, to pull on every time she felt as though she was weakening again.

She crossed the kitchen to the Tefal and poured herself a coffee. She added too much cream before she returned to the Nook. He looked at the coffee cup with disgust. She ignored his glance and its implications.

"Well, that's not the way it feels. You haven't gone into work, and you keep sighing and making faces at me. I wish you'd yell and punch and get it over with."

71

Her inner crazy was bubbling to the surface one word at a time like molten lava erupting into the ocean.

"You shouldn't be drinking that."

She looked down at her mug and remembered that she was pregnant. It was like when someone died, it wasn't on your mind all of the time, but just below it. Little things would suddenly bring the knowledge back to the forefront of your mind. Like cream in coffee. Or perhaps it was just the coffee. She realised that perhaps she should read the baby book she had bought, perhaps there were things she needed to know about being pregnant.

"One won't hurt," she replied.

He tutted; she rolled her eyes and picked up her mug.

"When you're ready to tell me what is going on in your head, you know where to find me."

She left him to mull over her new found confidence, curled up on the sofa in the lounge and turned on the television. The first channel had a daytime talk show on about violent destructive relationships, she turned the volume up to drown out his sighs and her own thoughts. She used the television to drown out the reality. She still thought he'd changed. Changed for good. She still worried because she knew the truth, but didn't want to believe. She had made her decision.

When her mug was empty and talk show number two was beginning, Max came to join her. He brought her two slices of toast and honey, a sweetened apology. The storm on his face had passed. He handed her the plate and sat down next to her.

"I'm sorry. I guess I was just so overwhelmed that I forgot about you and your emotions. I was angry that you didn't tell me the second you thought you might be pregnant, but I see your point of view, you did the right thing."

She bit into the toast leaving an impression of her teeth. There was so much honey that it dripped off, and ran down the inside of her wrist. She chewed slowly, digesting his words.

Her engagement ring turned on her finger, lubricated into its own movement by the honey. She turned it back to the correct position and without speaking, put her head on Max's shoulder. She continued to eat the toast. She didn't think she would be able to forgive him yet, so this halfway house would have to do. He put his arm around her; she felt his face change into a smile. She wished she could see what kind of smile, that way, she could be better prepared for the day ahead. They watched the end of 'I got a secret, and you ain't gonna like it!' together, giggling at the white trash. Not seeing themselves reflected in the lives on the screen.

She had a shower while Max put on the dishwasher. She didn't know what they were going to do now. They had watched television, they'd had breakfast, tidied up. There was a whole afternoon and evening ahead of them that they would have to utilise, and probably together. She grimaced at the thought.

"What's the matter?" Max asked as he came into the bedroom and saw her face in the mirror.

"Mascara went in my eye," she replied.

"Oh, are you ok?"

"Fine."

She smiled at him and hid the disgust of her thoughts at the back of her mind where even she tried not to delve.

"I thought we might go and look at houses." He dropped his bombshell.

"What?"

"Well, we can't live here with the baby, the garden is tiny and we only have one bedroom. I thought we could look for somewhere new. I can rent the flat out."

It made sense, but still she stared at him in disbelief.

"Ok," she said and continued with her makeup. At least now they had something constructive to do for the rest of the day. Something neutral they could talk about.

They discussed possibilities of where they wanted to live. Max wanted to move to Kent or somewhere south. He liked the

73

weather and the open space. Ruth was stubborn, refusing to budge. She would not leave the city to become a suburban housewife. They finally agreed to begin their search in W11 and headed out to find estate agents in the area.

They returned home with a pile of brochures and information. Ruth was shocked by the cost of houses, she didn't know how expensive they had become since she had last looked into it. She had thought the conversations they had at dinner parties were just politeness, she didn't realise that it was reality. She had forgotten about her house, about her ticket out. It was as though she had suppressed the knowledge for fear of what else she might know. The cheapest one they found was still one point eight million, and in Ruth's opinion, it wasn't even that nice. Max didn't seem to mind, he house-hunted at work every day. He made tuna sandwiches and they sat on the sofa to eat them with all the property brochures spread over the coffee table in front of them. The negative atmosphere had gone and they were talking quite happily together, sensibly discussing the finer points of each house, deciding jointly on which ones they wanted to view.

The phone rang.

Ruth answered it, leaving Max looking at a four-bedroom place in Notting Hill.

"Hello?"

No one spoke, just breathed, then the dead tone. She returned to the living room, still carrying the handset a la Ma Boswell. She placed it on her side of the coffee table.

"Must have been a wrong number," she said and tugged a brochure toward her.

"How about this one?" Max asked and passed her the information on a house in Mayfair. He was blushing.

She looked at Max. There was clearly something going on. He didn't meet her eyes, he continued to stare at the table, getting redder by the second.

"Were you expecting a phone call?"

"I'm sorry," he whispered, barely audible.

She stood up and went to the front door. She took his car keys from the phone table in the hallway and walked out.

Ruth got in the car and sat for a moment to see if Max followed her. She was surprised that he didn't, there was no movement inside the flat at all. She started the engine and drove south. She turned the stereo up full blast. She skipped through all Max's pre-loaded CDs before deciding on the radio. She didn't want him in the car with her. She drove down the motorway, not knowing where she could go. She had somewhere, but it was locked down in the cavern of her memories. Even when she passed the exit on the motorway, nothing stirred. She just wanted to get away. 'How could he do this to me? How could he?' she kept asking herself. Not once did she think about how she had done it to him. Her reasons had been valid, or so she believed.

She saw the turning signed for the South and took it. She drove and drove until she hit the sea. She arrived in Portsmouth and parked at the back of the funfair. The sea air was salty and rancid, but good for the soul, or so she had heard. She wondered why Max had not called her mobile, not hurled abuse at her down the electronic line to tell her that if she didn't come back that second, he'd kill her. Then she realised it was still in her bag under the coffee table.

Seagulls screamed annoyance at the public for disrupting their lives. The sea swept over the pebbles on the beach, cleaning and dirtying them at the same time. She wondered if, in the future, those stones would be sand. She wondered if she could just sit there and wait for that to happen. Her thoughts about his misdemeanour conflicted with those about her own. She lay blame and guilt in equal measures upon the strands in her mind, not realising that her actions had in fact been an attempt at escape. She should have left the car there and started a new life. From there, she could've gone to France or Spain, or even to the Police. She could've escaped before she cracked completely.

People walked past along the promenade, lovers hand in hand, tearing strips from her. Children ran, playing chase games with each other, trying to climb the balustrade that separated the beach from the path. Ice creams, plastic buckets and spades, chips in paper cones. She watched it all happen in the fading light. She loved the sea, loved the beach, loved the fair. The fair came alive as the sun finally set. Teenagers now walked in front of her heading for the neon glare and the safe fear of the rides, flirting in miniscule skirts and open-necked Ben Sherman shirts. She watched until the fair started to close. The decrepit sign announcing the presence of 'unusual gifts cards & decorative objects' disappeared into the shadows.

She realised that she was stiff and exceedingly thirsty. She scrounged some loose change from the ashtray and went into the pub next to the car park. She ordered a fruit juice. The rowdy punters shouted to each other about the music, the club they were headed to, the girls as they walked through. She used the facilities and left quietly.

She started the car and noticed that it needed petrol. She drove back out towards the motorway and refilled at the petrol station on the slip road, charging it to Max's fuel card. Her mind was as numb as her body. She steered north, travelling home. She wasn't sure it really was her home, but to her exhausted brain, it was the only place she knew she'd be wanted. She couldn't see she had any other choice.

She arrived in their street and the clock on the dashboard told her it was four in the morning. The flat was a blaze of light and she could hear music coming from the open windows. She parked the car and watched the shadows. She didn't know if she wanted to return. She should've run. Part of her thought that it might be time to leave for good and to try and make it on her own. She should have left them both. She saw Max's silhouette move across the light in the window. He hadn't even closed the curtains. She got out of the car and walked up the path. Her hands shook with the fear of

76

what she was about to face. She thought that perhaps if this time he took it too far, it would be the best thing for all of them, her unborn child included. She unlocked the door and walked in. She stood in the hallway, waiting. The lyrics of the song that had just begun washed over her.

Max came through the kitchen door on her right and stopped.

"I'm sorry," he said.

Not the greeting she had been expecting at all. Where were the fists? Where was the screaming and shouting? Where were her bruises and guilt? She said nothing, she didn't want to provoke him. Perhaps however, she'd now scared him. Perhaps there would be a longevity to the change because she had finally stood up for herself, all be it only for a few hours.

"Truly I am, I mean it. It was just a one night thing."

"Which night? Who was it?"

She tried to control her anger, rein it in, but the furrowing of her brow gave her away. If the relationship was to be saved, she thought, then she had to do her best to remain calm, to hide her feelings.

"The engagement night. Leanna. I was mad at you for not telling me, for allowing people to come over, for being the perfect hostess, for everything. She was just there with her red lips and sympathy."

"So it's my fault?"

"In a way it is. But, well, no, not really, I'm sorry, it's me, not you." Oh the irony, if only he had left to complete the circle.

"So what's going to happen now, Max? Who do you choose?"

"You of course, I've told Leanna that I won't see her again, unless she's with Fletch."

"Fletch was at the party, and that didn't stop you then!"

"I can't say to Fletch, when we go out tonight, don't bring your wife, can I?"

77

"Then maybe it's me or Fletch? Could you give up your best mate for your wife?"

She knew it would do no good, just make the rift bigger, make the inevitable punishment that much harder. There were two of her that she needed to consider, or so she thought. She was wrong however, there were three of her. The baby, Ruth sane and the Ruth that was losing the will to live. Three people, one body, it was never going to work. She walked into the lounge and sat down on the sofa.

The song playing on the stereo suddenly hit home as it drew to a close.

'But life still goes on. I can't get used to living without, living without. Living without you by my side. I don't want to live alone, hey. God knows, got to make it on my own. So baby can't you see. I've got to break free.'

And another part of her was destroyed, snapped. She felt disjointed, a contrivance in a contrived situation.

She stood up and walked past Max sitting on the floor in the hall. She collected his pillows from the bed and the spare blanket from the wardrobe. She threw them on the sofa. She turned off the stereo. She was sure the neighbours would have had enough of Queen by that time.

"We can talk in the morning," she said as she passed him for the final time.

She needed to get to the safety of the bedroom and lock the door before all the words that had ridiculously passed her lips in the last twenty minutes or so made it past his ears and into his brain. Once he thought about what she had actually said, she would be in for it. She'd like some sleep before that occurred.

He didn't look at her, he just hid his head in his hands. She went back into the bedroom and closed the door, shutting him out, locking him out.

11. Max

I'm sick of this. I sit here day after day, watching you, willing you to do *something,* anything. And nothing happens. The baby is doing fine. Healthy the doctor said, but he says you may have to have a caesarean if you don't wake up soon. I don't want that, I want you to hold our child, so bloody well wake up. If you love me, you'll wake up. I don't know what else I can try. I've sung to you, read to you, invited all our friends over to speak to you. I'm at a loss, what is going to make you open your eyes? Eight days. Eight long, long days. The doctor says that you're not brain dead, that your vital signs are good. That means you're still alive in there somewhere. It means that you can probably hear me. So here I go again, my daily mantra. I love you Ruth and want you to wake up. For God's sake, wake up.

I asked you to marry me straight after I'd slept with Leanna. It was more than just wanting to find out if you were pregnant to be honest. I figured that if you said no then I would make a clean break, because you weren't committed. If you said yes, then I'd end it with Leanna and make a real go of it with you. It was a test. Sickening. I should never have even considered leaving you. But you said yes and told me you were pregnant in the sweetest way. I was so excited. So happy. But then I thought you had lied to me, about not knowing when you did know. I was still wrong to have sex with Leanna again. You almost caught us that night. I was frightened you'd leave me. I was lucky though, wasn't I? You didn't catch us in the throws, but I'm almost sure you knew something was going on.

It nearly broke my heart when you found out. When she rang, that guilty phone call, and then I had to tell you.

I think Leanna gave me what I couldn't get from you, even though it was there in you the whole time. She told me she loved me, you never did. But then you showed me you loved me, doing really sweet things just out of the blue. Like that time you spent nearly all day learning to cook a meal so that you could give me a home-made dinner. That was really special. But she said the words. It was like being single again and just starting out in a new relationship. We dated, like I'd always wanted to do with you. But with you it just happened so fast, one day we met and two weeks later you'd moved in. We never went on dates, bowling, ice skating, the cinema. We just went from coffee to living together. It was scary, but I just figured it must mean we were right for each other.

Then there was Leanna, I got from her everything that I had missed with you. We went to pubs in the country, we went bowling, we went horse-riding. It wasn't all about sex. We rarely had sex. At first. Then she went mad. Told me that we were in love, I should leave you. And that night when you did leave. God I was so scared. I rang your mobile only to hear it ringing with that Kylie song you loved from under the coffee table. I felt so lonely. Leanna called. I just put the phone down each time. I couldn't speak to her because I knew if I did it would be over between us. My head was all over the place and the last thing I wanted to do was to confide in Leanna that you had left. She would have been over at the flat faster than Linford Christie.

I waited up for you, listening to your only two albums over and over again. It's just occurred to me, why did you only have two albums? Did you just listen to the things I liked to make me happy? Another thing to fix when you get out of here. I mean it Ruth, when you're better, we're going to make a real effort to get this relationship right. It might be hard work, but I love you, and I know you love me, so we can do it.

When you came back that night, I was so happy. I didn't ask where you'd been, or what you'd been doing. I found out later that you'd driven to Portsmouth because it came up on my fuel card that you'd filled up the car there. I mean that's a long way from home. It must have been really lonely in the car. I was grateful that you'd come back to me. I wanted to try again. I couldn't quite get there though. I couldn't say I would never see Leanna again. She was

80

like a drug, I was addicted and I needed her. I don't now though. I need you.

I'm trapped, waiting for you to see the light, to open your eyes, for crying out loud, move a finger. Fletch comes and tries to make me take a break, but I can't. What if I miss something? What if I don't see you making that effort I've been praying for? This is futile. I don't know what I'm doing here. Do you not want me to be here? Is that it? If I leave will you get better? What am I asking you for? You won't answer me. I can't cope anymore. I've become an insomniac, sitting here all through the night fixated on your hands, your lips, your toes, your eyes. And nothing. Nothing at all ever happens. Am I wasting my time? What do you want from me? I'm going to get a coffee, I need a break. I can't go on like this Ruth, I need you to give something back to me.

12. Ruth

She woke up alone in their king-size bed and wondered why it felt strange. Then the events of the previous evening, and early morning, ran through her mind like a film on fast forward. Sun was streaming through the gap in the curtains, so she figured it was very late. She looked at the clock and it said two. She lay watching the dust as it circulated through the light, preparing herself for Max. She couldn't put it off forever, as much as she wanted to.

She went to the door, and pressed her ear against the crack to listen for any noise suggesting that he was lying in wait for her outside. She could hear nothing except normal house noises and so braved opening the door. On the floor, blocking her exit was a huge bouquet of flowers. Nice ones for a change. Lilies, freesias, and a single red rose in the centre. A plush, two-foot tall teddy bear leant on the doorframe, it toppled forward as she opened the door further. She picked it up and a card slid from its paws.

She tentatively turned over the envelope. With a man like Max, you never knew what you were going to get. On the front he had written simply: Ruth. She opened it and pulled out the card. It had a picture of a 'Forever Friends' bear and written in a cute gold font, it had the legend 'I'm so sorry.' Inside Max had added, '...for all that I have done. I'm sorry Ruth, I love you and hope you'll still marry me, Max.'

Carrying the bear, she went into the lounge, searching for Max. The only clue that he had been there was the neatly folded blanket with pillows placed regimentally on top, at the end of the sofa. She went into the kitchen and there was another note under Charlie Chaplin. 'Breakfast in the fridge, have some stuff to do, will be home at about five. I love you, Max.' A lot of I love yous. It made her nervous. It made her worry about his plans for her, for later.

In the fridge, on the centre shelf was a bowl of fresh strawberries, ready to eat with a small carton of cream next to them.

82

She took the fruit and cream to the Breakfast Nook. She sat the bear at the end of the counter and began to peruse the house brochures still stacked there. She looked at house after house, not to decide where she wanted to live, but thinking about whether she wanted to live with Max.

She had a bath, waited for his return, killed time. The anticipation was driving her up the wall. Would it be an almighty show down where they fought irretrievably, or would it be the new calm Max, grovelling on his knees, trying to make things right again. Or would it be stilted where they just didn't really speak to one another. She honestly didn't know which would be worst, at least with the first option, she knew what she would be getting. She wanted to believe in option two though. Max really had changed this time. She smiled at the hope, but somewhere in the back of her brain, the idea that he could never and would never change gnawed relentlessly.

She wandered from room to room, tidying half-heartedly, not that it mattered, Max had tidied and cleaned already. He could be quite obsessive about cleaning sometimes, particularly if he was having a stressful time of it. She looked at their life together portrayed in the photos, the books, the CDs and the films. Her books, his music. She felt like they had never truly been one whole, only two disparate halves.

She continued to walk around the flat, room to room and back again, shredding the bouquet, leaving flower heads in her wake. Finally, when she was about to put the rose head into the fireplace, she heard his key turn in the lock. He came into the living room and looked at her. She returned the stare, analysing every shadow upon his face.

"Ruth, I'm sorry. I really am."

She didn't reply, she continued to watch his face, his poker face.

"I don't know how to make it up to you. But I will, just tell me what to do."

83

She didn't know what to say to him, what words would be safe or right.

"I went today and booked viewings on all the houses you liked, I've also booked us on a holiday. I thought if I showed you around Antigua, we could share it."

"I don't want to look at houses. I don't want to go to Antigua," she said.

"Ok, I'll cancel them, what do you want?"

She didn't know, she had nothing to say. She looked down at her nails, they were in poor shape, she needed a manicure, some pampering. Her mind blew away from the room, the situation. It moved elsewhere, somewhere where normality didn't matter.

"I'll do anything to keep you Ruth, anything at all. I want to fix this, my mistake, I want to make it better."

He reached out to her and gently caressed her cheek. She could feel the tension in his fingers, she wanted to shrink away from the touch, but it was too late. She looked up into his eyes. If only she had looked more closely before she'd allowed him within striking distance. She wanted to be loved, wanted people to stop leaving her. She didn't want him to know how she really felt, although, perhaps he could sense it. She wasn't angry; She was sad, miserable. Depressed maybe? People had left her all her life, but usually, She would prepare herself, watched for the signs, and then left before they could leave her. She had no idea with Max, she didn't expect this. *Maybe if I hadn't shut him out, things would have worked out. Maybe if I'd let him in No, it could never have worked, even now, I'm trying to convince myself to forgive his sins. I should leave that to the powers that be and use my own sense to run.* Max sighed, shuddering back imminent tears.

"I want us to be normal," she said. *Snap.*

"I want that too, really I do. I want us to be together forever and to have kids and grandkids and everything, a whole life." He tried to smile, tried to make everything fine again. She admired him

84

for that. She put her arms around his neck and pulled him to her. *Snap.*

"Never again Max, if there is a next time, I will walk," she whispered into his shoulder.

He's too close. I didn't see his eyes. He leant back to look down at her, his hand returned to her cheek, caressing it. He stepped slightly away from her, as though he wanted a better look. It is at this point that she realised all too late that he was seething.

"Leave me?"

Before she could respond, the hand that had been caressing her cheek had been pulled back and smashed forward into her cheekbone. Blooms of pain and light exploded behind her eye. She wobbled backwards, involuntary tears streamed down her face, followed shortly by real ones.

"You won't leave me," he said. "No one would have you."

He put his arms around her waist and his head on her shoulder. His tears trickled down her bare neck. Part of her, the part that was not shocked to the core, *how was I shocked?* was trying to understand how he was still upset about cheating on her when he had just that second given her a black eye. She couldn't pull away from him, she was not strong enough, but she didn't want to either. As much pain as she was in, she knew he'd make it up to her later. He didn't mean it, it was her fault, she had said the wrong thing.

Some time later, once he had put frozen peas on her eye, they lay on the sofa together, their legs entwined, their arms around each other. She felt that this was the right thing, and yet the wrong thing too. She thought, 'I should leave him before things get worse, before it happens again.' But she didn't want to live without him. She was carrying a child now, She had more than just herself to think of, and she couldn't be selfish. That should have given her the courage to leave, but it just made her stay. Max was a provider. She could now understand why Leanna stayed with Fletcher, why she would always stay with Max.

They didn't talk anymore, they just held each other like two lovers after sex. Max's breathing slowed. The bright light that came through the windows faded to an orange glow, and then to a dusky shadow. Again she made the first move. She got up and turned on the table lamps. She found the phone down the side of the sofa and called in a takeaway, she was so hungry. She curled up behind Max's legs on the end of the sofa and waited for it to arrive. Max went and put the plates in the oven, so that they would be warm for the food. The doorbell and the phone rang at the same time. Max took the door and Ruth answered the phone.

"Hello?"

"Ruth. Just the girl." It's Leanna.

"Get the fuck out of my life – and Max's."

"He loves me Ruth, he told me when he spoke to me today. The only reason he's staying with you is because you're preg -"

"You need help. I have to go now, Max and I are busy."

"I had sex with him today. In his car."

"Really," Ruth said.

"I left him a reminder, under the passenger seat."

She put the phone down. Ruth turned to look at Max through her un-swollen eye. He looked back at her puzzled. In repetition of the night before, she got the car keys from the hallway and went out the door. Max followed her this time, he was still carrying the bags of Chinese. She didn't even feel ashamed that the neighbours would see her eye. She could always say that she had walked into a door. They probably all knew what went on in the flat anyway. She walked bare foot, ignoring the stones on the pavement. She went to the passenger side and opened the door. Max looked at her as if she'd gone crazy. She wanted to look under the seat, but was too scared. She had made a threat, and if there was something there, she might have to follow it through somehow, even after the pain it had already caused her. The pain it would cause her. She crouched down and rooted under the seat. She pulled out McDonald's wrappers, receipts, a windscreen scraper. Frantic, she pulled

86

everything there into the foot well and sat on the seat so that she could search through it. She found what she was looking for, what she really didn't want to find. *Snap.*

"What's this?" she asked, holding up the necklace.

She opened the locket and inside there was a picture of Max and Leanna together. It appeared to show them getting married, but she recognised it as the photo from Leanna's wedding to Fletch, where Max was the best man. *Why best man, why not lying cheating scum man? Why not evil, violent bully man?* She started to cry, her tears dripped onto the smiling faces. Max watched her through the windscreen. He seemed confused. She got out of the car and locked it up again.

"Ruth? What is it?"

She gave him the locket and walked back into the flat without speaking. She went into the bedroom and locked the door once more. She couldn't face him. He knocked on the door, gently, tentatively, but she didn't answer.

"Ruth?"

She stayed silent.

He hammered against the door as if he was trying to break it down. He screamed her name. Everyone in the entire street must have been able to hear him. But then, they were probably as used to it as she was. She imagined them turning up the volume on their televisions as she tried to block out the noise coming from the door, block out the sight of it shaking in the frame. She imagined them sat there saying to each other, 'next door are at it again,' before returning to *Eastenders* and the pseudo-fictional lives of the characters.

With one last "I'll kill you, listen to me, I'll prove it to you!" Max stormed away into another part of the flat. She listened as he stomped back down the hall and into the living room. She heard him speaking, but didn't know who to, or what he was saying. Suddenly, his anger filled the flat once more, his voice thundering through the thin walls, only this time, it was not directed at her. *Little by little,*

87

bits snapped off me and died, but I didn't know that then. His words were amplified and clear, she listened to his one side of a conversation.

"Why did you put that locket in my car? When?"

"I told you, never again, I told you that it was a mistake."

"You really think I'd come running to you if she dumped me? You're crazy."

"Leanna, stay away from me and stay away from Ruth."

"Just keep the hell away from us. Fuck off."

He swore. Max would never swear at someone else, I used to pretend he never swore at all, but he did, if he was angry enough with me, but he kept that hidden from the outside world. He had a persona of wonderfulness to keep up. I should have guessed he was lying. There was no phone call. One fuck too many.

She heard Max coming back towards the bedroom. He knocked the door again, gentle and quiet once more.

"Ruth?"

She didn't reply. She heard the slither as he slid his back down the door. She imagined him sitting there, his knees bent, his head in his hands. She stood up slowly walked quietly to the door so she could listen to him. She could hear him breathing, deep, controlled breaths. He was calming himself down, he was trying to keep his fists in check. He started to mutter to himself, words she couldn't make out. He started to speak more clearly, talking through the door to her, knowing she could hear him. *Disembodied voices. And nothing has changed, has it?*

"She was lying Ruth. She put the locket there ages ago. I gave her a lift once. Before anything happened. She seems to have been planning to break us up for weeks. I have only had sex with her once, the time you know about. All the rest is lies." *Indeed. Everything that came from his mouth was a lie.*

She opened the door. Max, not expecting it, fell onto his back. She spoke to him looking down as he lay there.

88

"I believe you." She smiled down at him lying there helplessly. *Another snap.*

Some battles had to be lost for the greater good of the war. Max scrambled to his knees and she met him half way. They kissed passionately, lips locked, tongues tied, for what felt like hours, but could only have been minutes. They went back into the kitchen, the air almost clear between them, and sorted the Chinese out together. *Kiss me, kiss me. I haven't been kissed for forever.*

"We need to start again from the beginning, you know that, right?" she said.

"I know."

"You need to keep your fists to yourself, it's no good for the baby." She finally managed to bring his fists into the open. "Nor for me."

"I know that too."

They took the food into the living room and she allowed Max to show her the houses he had booked for them to see and the hotel he wanted them to go to in Antigua. She decided that she liked one of the houses a lot and thought that maybe a new start in a new home would be a good thing. She looked at the holiday brochure too. *The baby isn't ready yet I tell you. I'm only a few months pregnant, not even showing properly yet. No caesarean, no, I'm not ready.* The whole Antigua thing was too reminiscent of Leanna for her and she just couldn't bring herself to even consider going there.

"No problem," he said, and squeezed her shoulder, "we can have a holiday when the baby's born, anywhere you want to go."

"That would be better," she said, and lay aside the holiday stuff. She picked up the booklet for the house she liked again.

"We have to sort out wedding stuff too you know, like when we'll do the do, who the best man and the Maid of Honour will be."

"I want to get married before I begin to show that I'm pregnant. I think Fletch will have to be your best man, you were his," this was so difficult to deal with, there was so much she had to take into consideration, "and if he is your best man, Leanna will

89

have to be there. I want her under close scrutiny, I want to watch her every move so that she doesn't ruin anything. I want her to be the Maid of Honour."

Max breathed in sharply, as if her words were an actual blow to his stomach. She really wanted Leanna to suffer. If she was the Maid of Honour, she would have to spend weeks watching Max and Ruth showing off how much they loved each other and were preparing to spend the rest of their lives together. It would be painful, and she wouldn't be able to do anything about it because Fletcher would be there too. *I think I had finally completely and utterly lost it. If he had said to me that night, let's get married tomorrow, I reckon I would've done it. If he'd have beaten me unconscious, I still would've done it. My sense, what little I'd had, had gone absent without leave. I thank God that it doesn't seem to have been a permanent holiday.*

"Are you sure?" he asked.

"Yes," she replied, "But don't tell her or Fletcher. I want to break the news to her myself, in my own time." *Revenge, why couldn't I just let it lie?*

He smiled at Ruth and kissed her with a wet and mushy spring roll tasting kiss. She laughed properly for the first time in a long while. *And the last.*

13. Little Ruth

Ruth and Mam returned to the house. Mam sat at the kitchen table, her head on her arms and cried, her whole body heaving with each sob. Ruth patted her knee, and when that didn't seem to help, she dragged a chair over to the kettle next to the sink. She climbed up to stand upon the chair and got the kettle, filled it to the top with water and plugged it in the way she had seen Mam do it. She crawled along the worktop carefully so as not to fall and got out a tea bag and a mug. As she was crawling back, she dropped the mug, where it smashed into thousands of pieces on the solid kitchen floor. The kettle started to boil over because she had filled it up too much, and Mam still cried. Ruth sat on the work top between the kettle and the cooker and began to cry too. The tears washed her face in silence as hot water bubbled across the space between her and the kettle. *It could've been worse, I remember, when I was a bit older, I decided to help Mam by cleaning the kettle. I half filled it with water, added a dash of washing up liquid, and turned it on. It left a terrible mess, but Mam wasn't mad at me, she knew I'd been trying to help. That's why I loved her so much. She never got angry at me, she got angry, just never at me.*

Suddenly, a loud electrical crack came from the kettle.

"RUTH!" Mam screamed, shattering the sadness like it was no more than an elderly drinking glass.

She rushed across the room sending the chair flying out from beneath her and grabbed Ruth from the flooded surface where she sat. She ran up the stairs and into the bathroom with Ruth in her arms. She turned the cold tap on full and stood Ruth fully clothed in the bath. She snatched up the hair-washing jug and started pouring the freezing water over Ruth's bottom and legs. Still Ruth did not speak. *I was confused, I didn't have a clue what was going on.* The water felt nice running down her legs, making her dress sticky and wet. Mam kept muttering, "Oh Ruth," over and over again.

After what felt like forever, Mam finally stopped soaking her. She lifted her from the bath and removed her sodden clothes. She wrapped her in a big fluffy towel and carried her back downstairs to the living room where she laid Ruth on the settee and gave her the Clicker for the television.

"Thank God Daddy isn't here now, he'd be so angry. Don't worry, we won't tell him and I'm sure you'll be better by the time he next gets home, ay?" Mam said.

Ruth felt just fine, so she nodded to make Mam happy. She didn't want Mam to be scared as well as sad. She turned on the television to see if any Sesame Street was on as Mam went back into the kitchen to clean up the mess. Flicking through the four channels, she could find nothing she liked so she closed her eyes to have a snooze.

When she awoke, Mam was there, warming her nightie by the fire and it was starting to get dark.

"You're awake just in time for tea," Mam said when she realised Ruth was watching her, "I thought we might have pizza and ice cream as a special treat. How's that?"

Ruth was feeling rather hungry for a change, but still she asked, "Can we have it on our knees?"

"Of course. Tomorrow, we'll need to go and buy a new kettle, it blew up. We can get some shopping in at the same time and you can choose the veggies." *She was so cheerful about it all, she tried to create normality constantly, even though she couldn't. Not with Him in our lives.*

Mam left the room and Ruth got up and changed into her nightie. She folded the towel up and put it in Father's chair. Mam came back with her tray with a cheese and tomato pizza on her Starbright plate and they sat together watching the evening news.

A few days later, while Ruth was eating her Sugar Puffs, Mam told her they were going to do some very special shopping. She told Ruth that in just two weeks she was going to start big school and so she needed a uniform, a satchel and some school things.

Ruth contemplated this, she had been to nursery school the previous term, and had heard about big school from her teacher. She had said that in big school they sat at desks and did work and they didn't get to play so much. Ruth was not sure she really wanted to go.

Mam dressed her smartly and they went out in the car to town. They went to the special shop that sold lots of uniforms to lots of schoolchildren. It smelled dusty and like old sick and was very dark. *It's almost the same smells and atmosphere that traps me now. We think we forget these things, but they are never forgotten.* Ruth was frightened. They gave Mam a shirt, a tie and a tunic and showed her and Ruth into a curtained changing room,

"I don't like it in here," Ruth said.

"But you need to get your uniform so that you can go to school," Mam said. "Try it on and then we can leave."

Ruth put on the uniform with Mam's help and they left the changing room so that she could see her reflection in the big mirror. Ruth looked very smart and grown up. Her shirt was pale blue and she wore a navy tunic over the top of it. The tie was neatly done up with a proper knot and was blue and silver, it was tucked inside her tunic. Mam bought two tunics, three shirts, two ties and some white knee high socks with holes in them that made them look pretty.

Next they went to a Clarkes shoe shop where Ruth chose some navy shoes that were like her dolly's. They had a t-bar that did up on the side with a silver buckle and there were holes punched into the toe bit that made the pattern of a daisy. Ruth wanted to wear them home, but Mam said that she couldn't wear them until the first day of school. Then to make Ruth happy, Mam bought her the same pair in red so that she could wear them at home. *And that was the very last time that I had a new school uniform and new shoes. No wonder it plays through my mind. It was hand-me-downs from there on out. Bastard.* Ruth thought they had finished then, but they went

93

to another clothes shop where Mam bought her a nice warm navy coat and then they went to Woolworths. Ruth loved Woolworths because they sold toys as well as grown up things. Mam bought her a brown leather satchel with buckles on the front to keep it done up. She also bought her a Care Bears lunch box, a pair of navy mittens, a Care Bears pencil case, some coloured pencils and some normal ones and a fountain pen. Mam said that all the big children had fountain pens to write with, so Ruth could have one ready for when her writing was grown-up and joined-up.

Ruth had been really good all day. She hadn't wandered away and had only got upset a little bit in the shoe shop, so Mam bought her a grown-up doll for being so good.

"In for a penny, in for a pound," Mam said as she carried all the bits and pieces up to the till lady.

Ruth waited patiently while Mam paid and then they walked back to the car. Ruth held Mam's hand with her right; in her other hand she carried the bag with the grown-up doll. Maybe big school won't be so bad she thought as they crossed the car park. Mam had said that she had two weeks before she started. For Ruth, that was nearly a lifetime away.

When Ruth got home, she put on her new red shoes and went and sat in front of the television to play with her new doll. Mam had helped her read the name of the doll because she wasn't sure how it should be said. The doll's name was Barbie. Ruth pulled Barbie carefully from her box. She had boobies like Mam, but as far as Ruth could see, that was where the similarity ended. She brushed Barbie's hair with the little brush that had come in the box and then she dressed her in her evening gown ready for dinner. As Barbie wasn't a baby doll, Ruth felt she could really talk to her, so while she was waiting for tea, she sat telling Barbie all her secret fears about going to school.

Finally, the day came for Ruth's first day at school. Father had phoned her the night before and told her that he had paid a lot of money for Ruth to go to this school so it would be the best. *And how was that something I needed to know?* He'd said that if anyone was horrible to her then to tell him and he'd come home and sort them out. *And how was that appropriate for a young child to hear? One that lives with violence every, single day? I think he had been drinking, and thought he was funny, but he wasn't funny.* Ruth giggled and she told him about her new best friend, Barbie and about her new school uniform.

Ruth had her Sugar Puffs before she got dressed for school because Mam didn't want her to spill anything on her uniform. Then she got dressed in the clothes Mam had laid out for her on the radiator, only asking for help with the tie. Mam was very proud. They got in the car and arrived at the school ten minutes later.

Ruth looked out the window at the other children going in to the school and at the windows with pictures in them. Mam got out of the car to let Ruth out from the passenger side. As soon as Mam had closed the door, Ruth locked it. She had already locked her own door while Mam was distracted.

"Come on darling, don't be so silly," Mam said. Her voice muffled by the closed window. Ruth glared at her and got Barbie out from her satchel.

"How about, I go into school and ask your teacher to come and say hello? Would that be better?" Mam asked.

Ruth didn't reply, she was obstinately refusing to even look at Mam. She didn't want to see if she was disappointed, or even angry.

"I will not go into that place with all those big children," she told Barbie. "They'll hurt me and I won't like them and I don't want to do joined-up writing anyway."

Mam went into the school to find the teacher. While she was gone, a Father with his little boy came past. The boy was wearing a uniform like Ruth's, but instead of her cardigan, he wore a v-neck jumper and instead of a navy tunic, he wore grey shorts. The Father stopped by the car and looked in.

"Are you ok in there little lady?" he asked.

Ruth watched them from the corner of her eye, but wouldn't look up out at them properly.

"Let's get you into school and then I'll see if I can help the little girl. You be nice to her if she's in your class now won't you?" he said to his son.

Ruth saw the little boy nod and then his Father took him through the school gates. Ruth was shaking with fear. She didn't want a strange man trying to help her. She was just about to open the door when the man came back with Mam and another lady. Well, that settled it; she took her hand away from the lock mechanism and folded her arms across her chest.

"This is Mrs. Williams," Mam said. "She's your teacher."

Ruth looked over the lady carefully, watching for any signal that could mean she was a bad person, but she was smiling and looked very kind. This made Ruth scowl.

"My wife has the same car, want me to see if her key works on your lock?" asked the man.

Mam smiled gratefully, "That would be really helpful. My husband will go mad if I have to get the fire brigade out."

It was then that Ruth realised that the car keys were still in the ignition. She reached over to pull them out and Mam screamed.

"Don't touch the keys!"

The man was fumbling with his own keys, trying to find the right one. Ruth leant back into the seat and watched them. She could not understand why they were all so worried. She wasn't planning on moving the car, the whole point of locking herself inside it was so that she wouldn't have to go anywhere.

Finally, the man found the right key and tried it in the lock. The door opened and he laughed.

"What are the odds on that?" he said.

Mam laughed too and reached into the car for Ruth. Mrs. Williams got the keys for Mam and picked up Ruth's satchel and her Barbie. The nice man went back to his own car, Ruth frowned as hard as she could at his retreating back so that he would know her displeasure at being saved, but he didn't turn around.

Mam took Ruth into her classroom. It was very long and sunny because the roof was made of glass. All the children were running around playing games and a chubby, cheerful lady stood in the middle with the children that felt frightened like Ruth. Mrs. Williams showed Ruth her peg with her name on it and hung up her satchel and her coat. The little boy came over, the one that had been told to be nice to her, and introduced himself as Oliver and asked Ruth if she wanted to play with the doctor's set. Ruth wriggled down from Mam's arms and went off with Oliver without a backwards glance.

If only life could've continued that way. If only He had never returned and Mam and I could've lived on, happy and at peace.

14. Ruth

The world had moved on since then. Have I? She decided to have the wedding in her seventh month, knowing that she would be showing by then. She didn't want to do that, but then she realised how much more painful it would be for Leanna as she watched her walk down the aisle clearly carrying Max's baby. *His baby?* Leanna had been married to Fletcher for three years, and the one time Ruth had heard her mention children to him, at her and Max's engagement party no less, he had laughed loudly, braying in front of her friends.

"Why inflict you on a child? You're not the maternal type," he had said, much to the amusement of those around him, even Leanna mustered a smile.

Ruth sometimes wondered what went on behind closed doors. Perhaps, for Leanna, Fletch was just like that in public, and then at home, he was loving and kind. He might think being derisive in front of his friends was funny. The more Ruth thought about it, the more it was no real wonder she had gone after Max. Of course, he was the opposite. Loving and kind in public, and then at home, he was nothing of that ilk. Leanna didn't know that though. Ruth couldn't tell her and even if she did, Leanna would just assume Ruth was trying to put her off her husband.

At last, Max had changed, he no longer hit Ruth. For that, she was grateful. There were eight weeks until the wedding and sixteen, roughly, until the baby would be born. Ruth was scared for the child every time Max raised his hand, even if it was only to get a mug from the cupboard. She lived on edge, she just could not accept he was never going to hit her again, even though he hadn't done so for weeks. He worked from home a lot. He liked to stay with Ruth. He told her it was to protect her. Because he loved her. *In a way, we loved each other very much. I no longer have love for him. Only fear.*

She woke up on the morning of their anniversary to find he had left the room. She lay silently, hoping to hear silence. But no, she could hear his fingers tapping on his keyboard in the kitchen. She was sensitive to these sounds, they gave her prior warning. She could no longer ignore her bladder, so she got up to face the music. After peeing what seemed like her entire body mass, she went into the kitchen and poured a coffee for herself.

"Would you like a coffee?" she asked.

"You look a mess," he said.

"I've only just woken up, I'm having a coffee and then I'll have a shower and smarten up. Would you like a coffee?"

He looked over at her, malice in his eyes, in the turn of his mouth, in his posture. It looked as though this day would be a bad day. A really, really bad day. They had been together for three years. It was exactly eight weeks until their wedding. They should both be happy and loving. Celebrating their history and their future.

"You're letting yourself go. You look fat."

"I'm pregnant," she whispered.

"It's lucky I'll have you. No one else would even look twice."

She took her coffee back to the bedroom. Sat in front of the mirror, she began to cry. She asked herself, 'What has happened to me? Why can't I answer him back? Give him a taste of his own medicine?' She knew why. She was too scared. She used to take his fists and head butts and kicks thinking she deserved them, that there would be a reason for the outbursts, even if she didn't know what it was. All she could think now was that her baby did not deserve it. He, or she, was not a part of this. The child inside her had never met Max and therefore had never done anything that could give him reason to lash out.

The doorbell rang. She dried her eyes before going to answer it, she didn't want anyone to see she'd been crying, although nothing would hide the red rims and purple puffyness. She was still allowed to answer the door, even if she was no longer allowed out of it. She

99

had to do all her shopping and socialising online while Max was asleep, not that she ever bought much and she socialised even less. The odd Facebook like and an Ocado delivery were as good as it got. She felt it was easier that way. It also gave her a secret. She had passwords that Max could not even begin to guess. Although, they were all his name in one way or another. B@st@rd. W@ank8r. C0ck. She used numbers and symbols to disguise them even further, but there was no need, Max would never think of himself in those terms and would never even dream that Ruth did.

She opened the door as the bell rang a second time. She hadn't been quick enough. She heard Max mutter, "For Christ's sake," in the kitchen.

"Hi, can I help?" she said as pleasantly as possible to the delivery guy on the doorstep. Her fake smile was as uncomfortable as an enema, but what else could she do? She had to keep everything on an even keel and smiling did that.

"Delivery," he grunted and handed her a box with Max's name on it.

She smiled as brightly as she could and signed for the package. It was small, compact. She knew what it was, she had bought it. *I must have had plans, subconscious plans, even then. I had squirreled away thousands and thousands of pounds into a building society account. Every time Max gave me so much as a penny, I hid it, and then, when he was out, I ran to the branch at the end of our road, paid in whatever I had and ran back so that he wouldn't catch me. I also had my rental income. But I have no idea what's in my account now. I have people, secret people, that deal with that. Max knows nothing about it. I've never told anyone.*

"Too fat to get to the door before the guy had to ring again?" Max asked as she went through into the kitchen.

"I thought you had got it," She replied, she was barely conscious that she was pushing those unimaginable barriers that should most certainly be left alone.

"You do nothing around here, you're lazy, the least you can do is answer the door."

"Happy anniversary," she replied and held out the package to him.

He snatched it from her fingers with such force that one of her nails caught on the thick parcel tape and tore off. She didn't even flinch, it was as though she was dead inside, just a shell walking on more shells. She had strict rules to keep those shells intact. He took off the outer packaging, and then the wrapping paper. He didn't even notice that the pattern was personalised with their names and the date. He just threw it on the floor, leaving it for Ruth to pick up later. She loved companies online that offered gift wrapping. It kept her out of trouble, because she could just hand over the whole thing, and then he would be certain that she hadn't been out anywhere and that she hadn't opened his post. *I was a shadow of my former self, no, I think I was just a shadow.* He smiled at the message she had had written on the card, it was something she had thought long and hard about and she had made sure it was very loving and simpering.

'To Max, on our third anniversary, we've been through so much together, and now we have a wonderful future as a family. I can't wait to marry you. I love you, Ruth."

He opened the box inside and pulled out the watch. It was expensive, but not so expensive that he would moan. Something that was good enough for him to wear and to be seen wearing, but not so good that he would be angry. She had chosen it to mark the passing of their time together. She hoped he would get that. She didn't think he did. He looked at the watch, turned it over and over in his hands. Eventually, he took off his old watch and put the new one on in its place.

He came over to her, and she stiffened in preparation, her hands automatically covered her stomach, as if that would do anything to help. He was gentle, however, when he put his arms

101

around her. Tentatively, she reciprocated, breathing out slowly and steadily as she did so.

"I love you too Ruth," he said. "I always have and I always will. I don't mean those things I say to you, you're beautiful and I'm lucky to have you. Go get showered and I'll call Leanna and see if she'll go shopping with you. You need something new to wear to dinner tonight, now don't you?"

Just like that he had changed. It happened all the time. She often had days where she wondered if she had made up all the misery and violence. He was kind and caring, loving and sweet. In her mind, it made it all worthwhile. *I can't live like that anymore, never knowing if Jekyll or Hyde is going to meet me in the morning.* She looked up at his unconventionally gorgeous face and he kissed her gently, first on the tip of her nose and then on her lips. All the nastiness of the morning had been forgotten.

"Go on, get a move on," he said, smiling at her. He patted her bum affectionately as she turned to walk away. Ruth grinned at him over her shoulder and winked. He laughed in response. They were happy.

She continued to grin from ear to ear as she stepped into the shower and scrubbed herself clean of all the pain of the previous few days. They had been particularly harsh, more so than usual. There had been no respite from his remarks at all, not even in her sleep, because once she was there, she dreamed of him, and of her father, and she would hear their voices and words. She made herself look neat and tidy, but she didn't overdo it. Gone were the days of perfectly styled hair and lash extensions. Sometimes, if he thought she was too dressed up, he would tell her to go and change in case she attracted the wrong kind of attention. He loved her, she was certain of that. He just put his foot down on these things so that she would be safe on the streets of London, or so she reasoned with herself.

Once she was happy that she looked respectable, she returned to the kitchen, empty coffee cup in hand. He was sat back at the table, focused on his laptop. He seemed to not even notice her as she walked past him to the sink. She rinsed the cup and then placed it in the dishwasher, the way he liked, handle facing north. She noted that one of the plates wasn't in the right place. There was a gap between it and the one that came before it. She moved it so that he wouldn't notice. He had been particularly pernickety recently, and so she was being careful to keep the equilibrium. It always seemed so important that things were done correctly.

"Did you put the cup in properly?" he asked, as she had known he would.

"Yes," she replied as she closed the door.

"Leanna isn't free so she can't go with you."

Ruth's day crumbled around her ears. She could feel the drudgery slipping into place once more. She began to prepare herself for more time in front of the television, listening to the tap of his fingers as he worked in the kitchen. *Snap. When did the SNAPS start? I thought it was later. Perhaps it was that day, at that moment. Perhaps it was before then and I didn't notice.*

"I've ordered you a taxi instead. You have to get a taxi back too. I don't want you alone on the tube in your condition."

He looked up at her and smiled. It is the old Max. The man that, all that time ago, all those years, she had fallen in love with. The kind, loving beautiful Max. The one that never said anything mean, never raised his hands in anger. The one that never hurt her at all. The one that had saved her from a man that did. He came over to her, pulling his wallet from his back pocket as he did. He opened it in front of her and she was surprised to see that there were hundreds of pounds in that wallet. He never normally kept cash, he paid for everything with his card. *I'm not as random as you think I salad. Now where did I get that from?* He handed her three hundred pounds, or thereabouts. She wasn't sure of the exact amount, but it was a large bundle of twenties with a couple of fifties thrown in. *Money equals apology. Yet again. There has to be more than this in life.*

103

"This is for taxi fare, a new outfit, a haircut and some lunch. You take the whole afternoon. I'll see you back here this evening, when you're done. Oh, and just in case."

He handed her his credit card too and told her she could use it in an emergency.

"Just make sure you remember that new shoes do not constitute an emergency!"

Just as he kissed her on the cheek, the taxi beeped outside. *I could've gotten far away with all of that. Maybe even to Edinburgh or Aberdeen.*

"Thank you," she replied and kissed him passionately. She loved having the real Max back.

She left the flat and he stood in the doorway, waving goodbye as the taxi began to ferry her to Oxford Street. She couldn't keep the smile from her face, it would be there all day, it was just one of those smiles.

"You look happy love, having a good day?" the taxi driver asked.

"It's our anniversary," she replied, fiddling with her engagement ring. "I've been sent shopping with the credit card."

He laughed, filling the cab with sunshine. She watched the world go by with wonder as they journeyed to the shopping Mecca of the city. She couldn't believe this was happening. It was as though something had snapped *snap* inside of Max that morning. Perhaps he'd realised that Ruth really did love him and that she was ready to be his wife. Perhaps that was what had made him return to the man she had loved four years ago when they first met.

She spent the afternoon browsing stores for designer maternity wear. She stopped to get lunch at a little bistro where she could sit outside and watch the people toing and froing. She managed to get a cancellation at a hair salon and had her hair styled, feathered around the front, but only trimmed slightly everywhere else. Max liked her hair long. She had a fringe cut in too, the stylist convinced her that it was the latest fashion, and Ruth thought it

104

would suit her face. She even sipped at a glass of bubbly as the hairdresser did his work. Eventually, at about five o'clock, she hailed a cab to go back to the flat.

She lugged the bags into the hallway and listened out for Max's fingers in the kitchen, but there was no tapping. She put her bags down and checked the living room, she thought that perhaps he was snoozing on the sofa, which he sometimes liked to do if they had evening plans. He wasn't there, which left the bathroom or the bedroom. The bathroom door was ajar, which meant he was not in there. He liked privacy in the bathroom. If he was in there, she knew not to even to try and talk to him through the door.

She opened the bedroom door, a huge grin on her face, ready to leap on him in the bed and let him admire her new hair, but the grin turned to a grimace. He was there, and Leanna was astride him. The covers were on the floor, the curtains weren't even closed. She was naked, her large breasts with incredibly dark nipples, were bouncing as she bounced. Max's pale skin looked paler in contrast with her darkness. Ruth even noted that Leanna had a Brazilian. All this took seconds. Just seconds. They felt like a lifetime or maybe two. They didn't even notice Ruth standing there. They were both in ecstasy. Max had his 'I'm coming' face on. He moved his hands from behind his head and placed them on her hips, forcing her to slow down, taking control.

His hips bucked in tandem with hers, his fingers digging into her flesh. She would have bruises later. What would Fletch think? She cried out and her body seemed to spasm as the orgasm took over; Max's face was strained, all the muscles in his neck stood out. It happened at the same time, and Ruth was still stood there, watching. They smiled at each other and Leanna leant forward to kiss max. They finally see Ruth. She didn't even think about what they must have felt, seeing her there, watching. Although, it was clear to see what was going on in their heads, neither of them even tried to hide it from her. Leanna's face looked horrified, Max on the other hand, looked smug.

105

"Well, I wasn't getting any from you, and sex on your anniversary is traditional," he said, his eyes never left Ruth's. His hands never left Leanna.

Ruth turned and walked away. She went into the kitchen and gripped the edge of the sink. All she could think was that Max would kill her if she threw up in the kitchen sink. He'd batter her around the entire flat. She concentrated on breathing. Concentrated on controlling her emotions. Or emotion. She just felt sad. There was no anger. No pain, nothing at all, just sadness. She heard movement behind her, but she didn't turn around. She knew from the hushed voices and childish giggles that Max was seeing Leanna out.

"She'll be fine, I'll smooth things over," he said.

Ruth smirked, 'so Leanna needs consoling,' she thought. Not Ruth, but Leanna. She muttered something, but Ruth didn't catch the words.

"It'll be ok, honestly, you'll be having lunch with her again next week. I promise. Although, I don't think we should do this again, do you?"

She said something else and he laughed. It was a fun, happy sound. Not malicious or scathing.

"Yeah, it was a good one to go out on."

The door closed and Max came into the kitchen. He snaked his hands around Ruth's waist and placed them on her stomach. It was just as they settled that her baby kicked for the first time. It was a violent, almost angry kick, not a light flutter any more. *It didn't want him anywhere near us, that's why it was so powerful. I'm sure of it. I think my baby knew what was going on, and understood.* Max felt it too, Ruth actually saw it. Her stomach seemed to protrude as though an alien was trying to escape. She gasped, partially with the wonder, partially from the strange feeling. It was almost absurd. Max laughed and kissed her neck. It was as though he had forgotten that she had just found him in their bed shagging his best mate's wife.

106

"Is that the first kick?" he asked as he turned her around to face him.

She felt amazingly sick. Even if she wanted to answer him, she couldn't, in case she spewed the lovely tuna and sweet corn jacket potato she had eaten for lunch all over his face. *I should've done that.*

"I'm sorry, it was wrong, I'm going to change the sheets and clean the bedroom, you won't know it even happened."

Although what he said was apologetic, his voice was tinged with a warning that she could not miss. *He was telling me exactly what would happen. She wouldn't remember seeing him with Leanna. If she did, it would hurt. Everything she needed to know about that afternoon was in the tone of his voice.*

"Your hair looks lovely," he said and smiled kindly. "I'm guessing, as you look amazing, that I haven't any change."

He patted her bum and walked away, back to the bedroom. That was twice that day, a sure sign he was in a fantastic mood, and now she knew why.

"Dinner will be at seven," he called back to her.

She waited until he was safely in the bedroom before she ran the length of the flat to the bathroom. She hadn't been so sick since she had first been pregnant. The baby, as if it understood, made fluttery movements again once she had finished and was sat on the edge of the bath, her head in her hands. Max knocked gently on the door and asked if she was alright. She managed a fairly competent reply and blamed the vomiting on the movement of the baby. All the time, she rubbed her small bump in apology. She couldn't let him know the real reason, he would be livid if he knew she hadn't forgotten him and Leanna. At least he hadn't made her change the sheets, she thought, although, she was sure that they would be left for her to wash.

The phone rang and he went to answer it, the heels of his brogues clicking on the laminate of the hallway. She couldn't hear the conversation, but there was no need. He was quickly back at the

107

bathroom door to tell her that it had been Leanna wanting to know if Ruth would be free for lunch next week. He said that he had told her she would be. *Why didn't I leave then? Why? I went to dinner that night, dressed up in my new outfit. I went to lunch the next week with Leanna, who apologised profusely and promised that it would be the very last time. I think I'd truly gone over.*

15. Ruth

She hadn't seen Leanna for a while, not since the apologetic lunch. Leanna mentioned nothing of the wedding then. The entire conversation was about how sorry she was and how much she hoped Ruth would be able to see sense and not tell Fletch. Ruth felt that it wasn't about seeing sense exactly. It was more about keeping her mouth shut so that Max wouldn't permanently close it. That, Leanna did not know. Her apologies and pleads were wasted, Ruth already knew what was necessary for survival.

However, four weeks before the 'big day', Ruth called Leanna again and invited *her* out for lunch. She met her in a Starbucks as neutral territory. They just have coffee, she said she was too busy for anything more. The reality was that Leanna was terrified of spending time with Ruth, terrified that she might not just forgive and forget. Ruth knew how to broach the subject, but she still pretended to mull things over for some time as they sat there. She hoped the silence made Leanna feel uncomfortable. There was nothing she could do about Leanna sleeping with Max, not verbally, but she could play games too. Leanna stared into the depths of her cup and stirred the cappuccino incessantly, she built the froth into peaks and then destroyed them again. Ruth had decided earlier to adopt a simpering approach; she wanted to wrong foot her so that Leanna wouldn't know what was really going through Ruth's mind. *I hear them argue, Max says Leanna, I should have ended it when Ruth found out, and I'm sorry I didn't. And Leanna replies, but Max, I thought we were building something. No, I was destroying demons and going the wrong way about it. Go back to Fletcher, if he'll still have you. Almost the same as what Fletcher once said to me.*

"I think it's time to let go of the past. With the wedding only four weeks away, and Fletch being the best man, we need to make up."

She snorted, which created gaps in the surface of the froth, revealing the liquid depths beneath.

"I want this to be the best day of Max's life, and it will be ruined if there is tension between you and I." Ruth soldiered on, she was determined to win her over.

"Really?" she asked and looked up into Ruth's face for the first time. Ruth could see a love bite on her neck, in the shadow of her chin. She assumed that things must have been back to normal between Leanna and Fletcher. *It carried on? What do you mean it carried on? You lied to me. If only I could speak.*

"Of course," Ruth waited for her to fill the ensuing silence.

"Ok, bury the hatchet and all that." Her smile didn't quite reach her eyes; there was something almost malicious in her look.

"I'm glad you see it my way, Max and I want our wedding to be perfect."

She pressed her lips firmly together so that they almost disappeared, it looked as though she wanted to say something in retaliation, and it was taking all of her effort to keep quiet. *And now I know exactly what. It carried on.*

"I also want you to be my Maid of Honour."

She stared at Ruth, her lips full again in an open-mouthed tunnel. Ruth was delighted to see that she was speechless. Her mouth snapped closed, opened again, closed again. Ruth smiled at her encouragingly and prepared herself for the rebuff.

"I can't, what about… Why… No… Can't you ask someone else?"

"No Leanna, it needs to be you, you're the best man's wife, it wouldn't be perfect if I had anyone else. You can use the opportunity to make your amends, can't you?"

"Does Max know about this?"

"Yes," Ruth replied, although part of her thought that perhaps he had decided that she had forgotten the conversation they had had months ago. Considering recent events, he would probably be as surprised by this as Leanna was. *And life still goes on. New CD please,* Two Out of Three Ain't Bad *if you've got it.*

"Do I have to?" She sounded like a whining child who had just been told to eat sprouts.

"What would Fletch say if you didn't?"

She lowered her eyes and then abruptly looked back up, straight at Ruth, malevolently.

"I'll do it."

They went their separate ways. Ruth collected her pre-ordered wedding magazines from W H Smiths and took them home to peruse. She was looking for the ugliest bridesmaid dress she could find. There was little time left to order Leanna's dress, but luckily for Ruth, Leanna was a stock size eight. She would be able to buy anything she wanted off the peg. She was determined to find something that no one would ever want to wear. There were wedding photos to think of after all. Years of being able to look at Leanna and smile at how awful she looked.

A week or so later and Ruth received a text from Bethany, inviting her out for lunch with the girls. She hadn't had lunch with them since finding Leanna and Max together. She hadn't been able to face them; she was frightened that they all knew and had been laughing behind her back. She was so ashamed. She knew that Leanna probably hadn't said anything and that she was just paranoid, but still, she worried. She had so few friends, and no one she could trust. She was desperate for any kind of social interaction. Max was still letting her go out wherever she wanted, as long as she had told him all the details first, so she sent him a text and then replied to Bethany saying she would be there. She went and had a long bath in preparation. She relaxed by floating in the bubbles and talking to her bump. She left early so that she could go clothes shopping before meeting Bethany. Her bump was making it so that she had to leave the top two buttons of her jeans undone. She had very few maternity clothes as she hadn't been able to go out enough to buy

111

them. *His arms were too heavy. Whose arms? His. Mine are too, tell him I understand.*

It was the best thing that had happened since the Leanna and Max incident. Ruth had most of her freedom back. Max is difficult, but she was sure he would change, as long as she kept him informed all the time. The first sign of the change came the day after the 'event' when he went into the office. Since then, there had been no more working from home, and, even better for Ruth, she got her pocket money and could go out when she wanted to, she had to keep her phone on her, and she had to answer any calls or texts from him immediately, but she felt that was a small price to pay. She spent a lot of time shopping.

She went to Push and bought a pair of Bridgit Bardot jeans by Juicy Couture, a pale green tube top by Susana Monaco and a jar of Ultra Rich Anti-Stretchmark cream. It was her first proper maternity outfit and although the top was fairly impractical for the wintry weather, she couldn't resist. Up until now, she had made do with buying jeans the next size up and wearing baggy t-shirts she had bought online. Max would be pleased. It had been nice since he had gone back to working in the office instead of at home. Things had been normal, well, old style normal since. They laughed and joked more often, there was no meanness. He liked it when he came home and saw that she had been out shopping for the baby, or she told him that she had been out for lunch. He liked that she was in contact with him, and she never ignored his calls, that would make him worry.

She was excited as she got on the tube to Clapham South and made sure that the Push bag could be seen by everyone. She arrived at The Glow Lounge and found that Madison and Bethany were sitting at a table outside, basking in the weak, watery sun. Both were wearing puffed up winter coats. They looked like two beached whales. She walked up to them smiling cheerfully and chattering nervously about how good it was to see them and how she had missed them. She was scared that they would reject her because she

112

had been absent for so long. She sat down in an empty seat at the table.

"Should we wait for Laura before ordering anything?" she asked.

Bethany began to examine her manicure while Madison looked at her with a mix of sympathy and disgust in her eyes and sneer. After a few tense seconds, Madison spoke.

"Laura isn't coming. She says she couldn't bring herself to be seen in public with you after what you've done."

Ruth's jaw dropped. She knew that asking Leanna was idiotic, but she hadn't realised it would lead to animosity. *Snap.*

"What am I supposed to have done?" There was a pause, so she continued. "I guess I'll order now then, what are you two going to have?"

"We're not stopping long," Bethany muttered.

"Oh right, just me then." The waiter came towards the table and Ruth ordered an herbal tea. "So, what is she saying about me?"

Bethany finally stopped admiring her manicure and looked at Ruth. "Ruth honey, everyone is really mad that you didn't choose one of us."

"We only met you today to see if you regretted it at all," Madison was barely able to control her anger.

"Max and I talked it over and agreed it was the right thing to do. She's Fletcher's wife, and he's Max's best man …" Ruth was bewildered, she had never considered these women to be friends, they were just the wives of Max's friends. She socialised with them because that was the expected thing to do, not because she liked them. *If only they had known the whole truth of it.*

Bethany took hold of Ruth's hand in both of her own. "Just tell Leanna you changed your mind, she's really upset you know. She doesn't know what to do for the best, but she feels like you're pressuring her into doing the wedding."

Ruth snatched back her hand and jumped up so quickly that her chair tipped over.

113

"That's none of your bloody business. And I'd be glad if you didn't gossip about me when you haven't even had the grace to ask for my side of the story ..."

She grabbed her bags and with tears doubling her vision, she ran straight into the waiter, who poured her tea over his foot as she knocked him. She fell off the curb, twisting her ankle and landed on her bum with a jarring shock. Her bump kicked back in protest.

She heard Bethany behind her sigh, "Oh Ruth."

She got back to her feet before anyone could help her. As she stumbled off, Madison called after her, "Leanna said he was crap in bed anyway. She says you're welcome to him."

"Leave her alone," Bethany snapped.

Ruth began to run. She arrived at the tube station out of breath. She searched for her mobile in her handbag, she wanted to call Max, her knight in shining armour. A car pulled up at the curb in front of her, but she only gave it a cursory glance as she scrabbled through her handbag paraphernalia. A shadow blocked the light, she was annoyed as she needed to continue her futile search. *Squeeze my hand Ruth, good girl, well done. Did she do it? She did it! She's getting better.* She looked up into the deep brown eyes of Fletcher. He grinned at her as though they were old friends.

"Can I help a maiden in distress?"

"I'm fine, or at least I would be if you would move out of my light."

He stepped aside, but he didn't go away. He continued to watch her as she searched for her phone. She could feel heat rising up the side of her face under his glare. She gave up on her attempt to find her phone and started looking around for a phone box.

"Can't I offer you a lift anywhere?" *Down in the dungeons.*

"No, thank you."

"I saw you and I thought I'd stop to say thank you for not telling Max, and letting Leanna be involved in the wedding. It's really made her really happy."

She looked at Fletcher, she was bemused in many ways. "That's not what I heard, have you told her about what happened, between us?" Or has she told you about her own antics? But Ruth didn't ask that question. She knew her place in the soap opera that was her life.

"No, why? She told me last night how much she is looking forward to being Maid of Honour."

"Oh, well, I was going to call her tonight and tell her not to bother, I just had Bethany and Madison giving me a lecture, telling me that Leanna doesn't want to do it and can't cope with the pressure I'm putting on her." Inwardly, Ruth was giggling like a little girl in the playground.

"Those two bints? They don't know what they're talking about," he said. He frowned and then with a furtive glance around him, he continued, "Listen, I put two and two together. If it is mine, then I'll give you money and stuff if Max doesn't stand by you. But Leanna is never to know. She can never ever know. And I don't want any contact with it, ever."

"That's fine Fletch, and for your information, the baby isn't yours." *I think it might be his. I'm almost sure that's how the ricochet inside my brain began. Although, I'm not allowing for the anguish of being with Max. It was probably a fifty-fifty thing.*

"Thank God for that," Fletch smiled with obvious relief, "I was so worried. Come on, let me give you that lift home."

"I'll take the tube." *So many different types of tube. The one up my nose could do with being taken.*

She went into the flat and closed the door behind her. Her heart hammered as though she had been running a marathon. She caressed her distended belly, feeling the way her belly button was starting to change shape, and slowly, her heart returned to its normal pace. She decided that all the herbal tea she had been drinking just wasn't doing her any good and so she made herself some coffee as a treat. She went into the lounge and curled up on the sofa. She read the next chapter in her baby book as she sipped her extravagant drink.

She couldn't concentrate. Fletch was like he had been when they had first met. Like he had been the first night of the party when Max was away. She just felt sorry for him and Leanna. She smiled at her newfound peace with it all. Sod the girls. *We'll have to do it soon Mr Parker, or the baby will die. Just one more week, please, she's made progress. One more week and then we'll have to. Wake up Ruth.*

She spent the afternoon teaching herself to cook spaghetti puttanesca with the aid of Delia Smith. Her first attempt was a solid mass, and both the pan and the mixture ended up in the bin. She had to learn, she thought, or else how would she ever feed her child? She had prepared for disaster, and had bought plenty of ingredients so that she could keep trying. The second attempt had the consistency of wet concrete, but it was better than the solid concrete of the first. Finally, when Max got in from work and after another failed attempt, *they have been extremely worried* she had it just about right.

"Something smells good," he said as he came through the front door.

She heard him clambering over the boxes of their belongings that littered the hallway ready for the move straight after the wedding. He walked up behind her and snaked his arms around her waist as she continued to stir the puttanesca.

"Did you cook that yourself?" he asked. She nodded in reply, quietly proud of her efforts. "It looks good."

He kissed her neck on about the same spot as where Leanna had her love bite and then went back to the hall to take off his coat. *The same, always the same.* Ruth served up her creation and took it to the Breakfast Nook. She had laid the table properly, with napkins, fresh rolls and butter curls on side plates, a single rose in a long stemmed vase and an open bottle of wine. He came around the corner and stopped.

116

"What's all this in aid of?"

"I wanted to make a show for the first time I cooked, so I have."

He sat down and smiled at her. She could feel rather than see his pride, it emanated from him like heat from a boiler. The meal smelt delicious and she was amazed that she had made it herself.

"Well, let's tuck in," he laughed.

"You go first," she said.

She wanted to watch his face as he took his first mouthful. She wanted to see if she had truly succeeded, or if he would eat it just to be polite. He picked up his cutlery nervously and swapped the knife and the fork over. She always forgot that he was left-handed. He carefully selected the first bite and raised it to his mouth. He smiled at her again, but this time he looked worried. As if he was about to eat poison. *Why didn't I think of that before?* He started to chew, and his face gave the information she needed.

"This is excellent, how long have you been hiding these culinary skills of yours?"

"I learnt today, the proof, if you need it, is that we need a new pan set. I had to throw away a fair few pots."

He laughed and reached over to pick up her hand. He kissed it, leaving an orange grease mark.

"Bless you," he said.

They talked about their day. He told her who was doing what or whom at the office, and she told him the details from her lunch with the girls, and most of what was said when she saw Fletcher. She left out the discussion about the parentage of her bump. Max was instantly angry with Madison and Bethany and said he would speak to Phil and Marcus the next day. It made her happy. He was taking her side in the disagreement. He was protecting her. It was when he did these things that she knew he loved her, and that he had changed at last.

He told her to make an appointment with the hospital to check her bump was ok. She agreed to stop him nagging her, but she

117

knew she wouldn't go, she was certain that her bump was fine. *When did I start referring to the baby as Bump. I don't remember, but it worries me. When did I start to forget that it was a human being and was in danger, as much danger as I was.* They retired to the lounge after dinner, and snuggled up on the sofa. Max wanted them to make love, but she was worried about the baby. The book had said it would be ok, but she wanted to be safe. He looked disgruntled, but took her decision fairly well. *Surprisingly well. Or not, in light of new information.*

"Only two and a half more months," she said, hoping he saw this as a light at the end of a tunnel. *I think I see the light, oh it blinds me. Her reflexes are improving.*

16. Little Ruth

Ruth had a fantastic time at school. She made lots of new friends; they played games together and did painting. At lunch, she decided that she didn't want to have packed lunches anymore because the school dinners looked so yummy and none of her friends had packed lunches. In the afternoon, they did quiet activities. The first was reading and Ruth, who could already read, was sent to the biggest class with a note for the teacher so that she could have a big children's' book. She had read her picture book in about five seconds, but she enjoyed the story about Topsy. Finally it was home time, they were all given spellings to put in their bags ready to learn at home and everyone got to take a book to practice reading. Mrs Greenwood sent them out into the playground while they waited for their parents to arrive. Ruth played "What's the time Mr Wolf" with her new friends until she heard Mam call her name. *Up until that moment, or perhaps until slightly later that afternoon, that had been the best day of my life. It truly had.*

She ran to Mam, her satchel bouncing on her hip, shouting for everyone to hear, "I forgot my knickers! I had to borrow some!"

Mam looked mortified at this piece of news, but she still had a tentative, carefully drawn smile for Ruth. Just as she reached Mam and started gabbling about her reading and her painting that was too wet to bring home so it was on the washing line and she'd show it to her tomorrow, Father stepped out from behind Mam. He hadn't really been hidden, but Ruth was too excited to notice someone she wasn't expecting to see.

He crouched down to her height and said, "Hello Sweetheart."

Ruth ran to him and flung her arms around his neck, nearly knocking him over, Mam forgotten. *And guilt for that moment has lived with me for every single day since.* She started telling him all her news from the day as he scooped her up and took her to the car. Mam followed silently behind. *I was bright enough to notice, but I missed each and every warning sign.* Father sat her in the front passenger seat and went around to the driver's side. Mam sat in the back behind Ruth.

"This calls for a very special treat," he said as he started up the car.

Ruth chatted excitedly about her day as they drove along, Father laughed in all the right places in her stories and was very sincere when Ruth told him about the seriousness of reading a big kids' book. Mam was silent. Eventually, he pulled into a car park of a place called Toys R Us. Mam helped Ruth get out of the car and she looked up at the sign. It had a big Giraffe on it and the "R" was back to front. Ruth pointed this out to Father as she took his hand and they walked towards the doors, she knew it would please him and he was in such a wonderful mood that she wanted to keep him that way.

He laughed and turned to Mam, "She gets it from me."

They went in through the doors and Ruth's eyes lit up. There were rows and rows of tall shelves that she had to crane her neck to see the tops and they were packed solid with toys. Nothing but toys. Ruth turned back to her parents who had stopped to watch her amazement.

Father said, "I'll get the trolley and you get the shopping, you can go off on your own, but don't leave the shop. If you find anything you want, bring it back to me and Mummy, right?"

Ruth nodded and ran off at full pelt to the first aisle.

17. Little Ruth

It didn't occur to her to wonder why she was being so spoilt or why Mam was so quiet, the overwhelming awe had knocked all her normal sensitivity out of her head. She ran from aisle to aisle choosing new Barbie dolls, Zapf Creation dolls, accessories of dolls clothes and prams and cars. She picked up a Princess outfit for herself and a swimming pool for Barbie. Finally, when the trolley was nearly full, she found a lilac bike with an oogah horn and shiny streamers that flowed from the handle-bars. Father made her have some stabilisers if she was going to have the bike, but it was still beautiful. She had never ridden a bike before and was completely unable to control her excitement. She was leaping around the checkout as Father waited to pay. *So much consumerism, so much materialism, and none of it solved anything, did it? I was too young then to understand, although I did associate gifts with the word 'sorry', but I'm not now, so why did I not see Max doing the same thing? The same kind of apology that is empty and worthless.*

"Behave yourself or you aren't having any of it!" Father shouted, his whole mood destroyed in a split second.

Ruth stood still and reached for Mam's hand. She looked up at Mam and noticed her sadness for the first time. The thumb from her free hand surreptitiously found its way into her mouth.

Father didn't speak again until they were in the car. He apologised to Ruth for shouting, but said that she must behave more like a lady in public in the future because she was a big girl at school now. She was sitting in the front again, and she suddenly wondered why she was in the front and not Mam, but then Father put the radio on and started singing along to it, trying to get Ruth to join in. *Always the same, change, then change, then change. Never a constant. I'll have a constant please Carol.* She let go of the questions in her mind as she giggled with her Father and sang along to Gary Glitter.

When they got home, Father told Mam to take all the toys up to Ruth's bedroom while he dealt with the bike. He put the stabilisers on it and pushed it over to the car park with Ruth following. She didn't really feel all that happy about being alone with him, but the bike held too much fascination for her to refuse. He spent the rest of the afternoon teaching her to ride it. They had lots of fun together and he kept telling Ruth that she was wonderful and she was the best girl in the world. By the time Mam called them in for tea, Ruth was able to ride her bike without him holding the

121

back, but she was still a little wobbly. He had made her feel special, better than everyone.

After tea, they sat on the settee, Mam one side and Father the other. Father had put on Doctor Who and as the opening credits started, Ruth curled into a ball between them to watch through her fingers.

"Do we have to watch this? She's scared and she'll be up all night with nightmares," Mam said.

"Shut up woman," Father replied and he swung his arm around in a high arc above Ruth's head, smacking Mam squarely across the mouth.

Mam's lip split open and she cried out as blood started to pour down her chin. He put the same arm around Ruth gently. He flicked his eyes over the battered and stunned face of Mam.

"Go and get cleaned up, you disgust me."

Mam left the room, hiccupping with suppressed sobs. Father sat quietly watching Doctor Who with Ruth at his side. She thought Mam must have done something really wrong to make Father hit her when he was sober. She just couldn't figure out what it had been. She felt safe though, she knew she was his best girl and that he would never hit her like that. If she wasn't then why would he have bought her all those toys? Why would she have a brand new bike that she could nearly ride on her own?

Mam didn't return to the living room when she came down the stairs, but busied herself cleaning up the kitchen. Ruth could smell the sharp lemon Jif that Mam used and could hear the quiet chink of plates and cutlery being washed over the sound of the television. She secretly thought that it would be best for Mam to stay in the kitchen if she was going to make Father upset.

Finally, when it was really dark, Father picked her up and took her upstairs to bed. She changed into her nightie and he watched while she brushed her teeth to make sure she didn't miss any. He tucked her in under her duvet, ruffling her hair before removing her thumb from her mouth. He didn't like her sucking her

122

thumb, he said that was what babies did and that she wasn't a baby anymore.

"You know that whatever happens, you're my best girl and I love you very much," he said

"I love you too Daddy."

She put her arms around his neck and inhaled his smell of old cigarette smoke and warm aftershave.

He switched on her Rapunzel night-light and left the room. As he was closing the door, Ruth thought his cheeks looked rather shiny and wet, but she had had such a wonderful and tiring day that she just closed her eyes and went to sleep straight away. She didn't stop to think about why things had been so unordinary all day and why Mam and Father had looked so sad this evening, or why Mam had made Father mad enough to strike out at her. She dreamt of Father teaching her how to ride her bike without stabilisers and cheering her on as she went faster and faster.

The following morning, Mam came to wake her up. She got dressed carefully, remembering to put on her vest *and* her knickers and went down stairs with her tie in her hand. She chose Shreddies for breakfast and Mam tucked a tea towel under her chin so that if she spilt any, it wouldn't go on her uniform. She sat staring at her breakfast until the milk had made the cereal soggy. Mam asked her why she wasn't eating her breakfast, because she'd be late if she didn't hurry.

"I'm waiting for Daddy, is he still asleep?" Ruth asked.

"Daddy had to leave last night after you went to bed," Mam answered slowly, as though she was trying to think of the best way to speak.

"But he didn't say goodbye," Ruth said.

"He said to say goodbye and that he loves you very much."

"When will he be back?" Ruth's voice was strangled by the beginnings of tears.

"Daddy will be away for a long time this time, so I'm not sure." Mam said.

123

"Can I phone him and ask?"

"I don't have his telephone number."

Mam's voice cracked as she spoke and she turned away to look out the window over the sink; she was shaking. The corners of her mouth dipped down, reopening the split in her lip from the night before and the blood and salty tears dripped pinkly into the empty sink. Ruth started to cry too. She didn't understand. Yesterday, Father had told her that she was his world, and today he had gone. *Everyone goes somewhere eventually. Some people just don't go soon enough.*

Mam finally stopped crying and went upstairs to wash her face and clean up the mess of her lip. Ruth refused to touch her breakfast. They drove to school in silence. Mam had tried to talk to Ruth, but she refused to speak so Mam gave up. When they arrived, Mam took Ruth right into the classroom as she had on her first day. Ruth held Mam's hand tightly as she listened to her talk to Mrs Greenwood.

"Rick left us last night. Hannah is in a real state of shock, she hasn't eaten her breakfast and she won't really talk," she said to Mrs Greenwood.

Mrs Greenwood took hold of Ruth's other hand and said, "That's alright Valerie, we'll look after her."

Then she turned to Ruth and said, "You can be my special helper today can't you?"

Ruth tried to smile at Mrs Greenwood, but her mouth kept turning the wrong way, so she just nodded. Mam left the classroom and Ruth went over to sit with Mrs Greenwood in the quiet corner. Mrs Greenwood had chosen a new book for Ruth and explained that this was a very big children's read and so she might not know a lot of the words, but Mrs Greenwood had thought she might like to try. Ruth looked at the book, it was called *The Magic Faraway Tree*. She opened it to the first page and snuggled in next to her teacher on the beanbag to read. *And there began my escape route. The one place I would always be safe and where no one would leave me without there being a build up first so that I was prepared.*

Ruth didn't play all day. She spent her time with her new book in the corner. Mrs Greenwood had told the other children that Ruth wasn't very well and so she was sad. In the afternoon, Oliver made her a glitter picture of a smiling face to cheer her up. She said thank you and then went back to her story. When home time came, she stayed in the classroom for Mam to come and collect her instead of playing outside with the others. Mam had a very long and serious conversation with Mrs Greenwood while Ruth stayed in her corner, and then Mam got her coat and took her home. She didn't speak to Mam for the rest of that evening. She didn't eat, she just lay on her bed staring at the glow in the dark stars on her ceiling. Father had put them up there on his last proper stay at home. She watched them through eyes blurred with tears.

18. Ruth

I want to live, I've decided. The morning arrived when Leanna and Ruth were going together for the final dress fittings. Leanna had been acting contrite recently; Ruth thought that perhaps Fletcher had spoken to her. However, she felt sure that this trip would change all that. *Or maybe it was Max in one of his private sessions with her.* Ruth picked her up outside her apartment in a taxi. The concierge held the door open. Ruth made sure she caught his eye and winked. The look on his face as Leanna got in next to her was priceless. It set her off in a fit of giggles that she could not control. Leanna sucked her teeth in a seething sneer. It seemed that she was already in a pretty foul mood. Perhaps it had been Fletch having a word with her and that had got her riled. Ruth doubted that Max would've said anything now she thought about it. Not only had he sworn that he hadn't spoken to her since The Incident, which was how he referred to the day Ruth found him shagging Leanna in their bed, but also, he would see it as girls' stuff and leave them both to it.

Things had been going really well with Max recently, so she was not going to bring it up again. He had been loving and kind, although she had been difficult in her opinion. She had only been punished because she had forgotten about putting the mugs in the right way in the dishwasher. And then one more time, for stealing the quilt in the night when she was asleep. And then the day before, when she did not answering her mobile quickly enough. She had forgotten about that until he came home from work. She couldn't forget now. Purple bruises covered her thighs and lower back, although the only time it hurt was when she was walking, or when she sat for too long and got stiff. He was right though. 'I deserved it,' she thought. Afterwards, he had said he was sorry that he had to punish her, but that it was the only way she would learn. *I never learnt and I certainly didn't deserve it, what the hell happened to me?*

"I'm sorry, it's the hormones, little things and I just lose control," she said, forgetting all her memories and returning to the situation in the car, Leanna was still tutting at her in annoyance.

Ruth watched her from the corner of her eye, as she rolled her eyes and sucked her teeth again. She tried to control her giggling, but the more she suppressed the laughter, the more it bubbled. She was nearly choking on holding it back, tears streamed down her face. Ruth couldn't quite work out why Leanna was so pissed off, but she didn't care, that was what kept the laughter going, it was her anger. *I must have been mad, to be so excruciatingly happy while all that was going on in the background.*

"Oh for crying out loud girl, get a hold of yourself. People can see us you know."

Ruth started to laugh loudly and raucously *hysterically*; she doubled up in the back of the cab, she could no longer see out of the window from the tears that fogged her eyes. Leanna huffed and puffed from the passenger seat next to her. Slowly, Ruth managed to calm down, but she could feel the giggles at the back of her throat, just waiting for the next thing to set her off.

"Seriously, it's the hormones." She thought about adding, 'I have to pee a lot too', but that made her feel like laughing again, so she pressed her lips together and bit back the words.

They finally arrived at the dress shop. For Leanna, it would be the first time she had seen the dresses. *I see your shadow, I see a misty light and you walk through.* Ruth was wild with excitement, she could not wait to see Leanna's face when she saw her gown. Ruth had chosen a cut for Leanna that would make her bottom look even bigger than it already was and would probably add five pounds to her hips. The colour complemented the accessory colour on Ruth's dress, but it would clash violently with Leanna's hair and skin. She wanted her to look terrible without it looking like that was what she had done. Leanna's dress was perfectly coordinated with her own; it just wouldn't suit Leanna. It was Ruth's day after all, she had to look the best anyway. *I have issues.*

127

Leanna sat silently while Ruth was hidden in the changing room. It took time to ensure her voluminous, beautiful dress was put in place. Ruth didn't see the look on the girl's face as she gently settled the dress over her battered body. She didn't hear the whispered conversation when the girl asked if Ruth needed help, if there was someone she could call for her. Like the police. Ruth responded that it had been her fault, she had slipped on the stairs. Max had been careful in doling out her punishments, and so once the dress is on, everything that shouldn't be seen was hidden. The girl smiled sadly at her and then took her outside for the final adjustments that needed to be made to accommodate the growing bump.

The wedding was in a week's time. She stared down at her deformed figure and hoped it wouldn't change any more in the last seven days. The assistant was full of praise and joy as she noted down the details of the latest adjustments. It was false, Ruth knew it was, because she could still see suspicion in her eyes, but she was a fine actress.

"Doesn't she look just wonderful?" the girl asked Leanna.

"Hmm," Leanna replied, her eyebrows arched just enough to convey her disagreement.

Ruth smirked to herself as she returned to the cubicle to change back into her maternity daywear. She came out and swapped places with Leanna. She looked happier, it was as though as soon as the attention was focused on her, she became this ideal butter-wouldn't-melt woman. The assistant followed her into the cubicle to help her into her wedding day outfit. Ruth had insisted that her Maid of Honour was to wear her dress all day, including through the reception in the evening. Leanna was fine with that when Ruth first mentioned it, and then later laid it down as law. Ruth waited patiently.

After some time the shop assistant came out of the cubicle. She walked over to Ruth, her eyes twinkled nervously.

"I don't think she likes her dress," she said.

On another day, in a different lifetime, Ruth thought that this girl could be very good friends with her. She was caring and kind, and quite clearly had a wicked sense of humour. Ruth put her hand to her mouth to stifle the fresh bought of giggles that were trying to escape. The shop girl bit her bottom lip in a clear effort to remain composed. Ruth couldn't look at her, she knew that if she caught her eye, then she would be done. Ruth would be laughing uncontrollably for hours on end. *I will smile today, I know I can do it, the corners of my mouth twitch expectantly.* She couldn't bring herself to say anything to coax Leanna from her cubicle. She knew that it would keep her in there for longer if she snorted her way through some pathetic excuse for friendliness. Ruth kept quiet and listened instead to the annoyance issuing from behind the curtain. Leanna was cursing her from here to oblivion, and she knew Ruth could hear, but she no longer cared.

A lot had changed between them. Leanna was no longer pathetic and simpering, apologising constantly. She was now irritated and antagonised. Ruth thought that she was jealous of her and Max. She thought that perhaps she had been expecting him to leave her to be with Leanna, to get her away from Fletch. *She's welcome to him, although I wouldn't wish that man on my worst enemy.* She didn't seem to realise that she was just a fuck to him. He wasn't getting any from Ruth, so he had gone to the next, easiest available, source. That just happened to be Leanna. Ruth was determined that Max loved her and the once the baby was born, things would be different. Everything he said and did showed that. Leanna didn't stand a chance.

Eventually, Leanna emerged, bracing herself to look in the main mirror. Trepidation was on her face, as if she expected it all to look so much worse once she could see it in its glorious entirety. And she was right. The cut of the dress was perfect; a fishtail style with padded puffed out shoulders. It made her breasts look smaller and her bum look like that of an elephant. Ruth had teamed it with flat satin shoes so that Leanna didn't even have a stiletto to lengthen her leg. She looked quite dumpy. Ruth smiled pleasantly, as though she was looking at her in a different dress to the one she was wearing.

"The colour is a bit bright," Leanna said, twisting herself around in front of the mirror.

"But it had to be that shade of turquoise to match the flowers on my dress," Ruth replied.

"The shoes are all wrong, I've a pair of my own that'll go better. With heels"

"But you have to wear them, the embroidery goes with the dress."

"I can't walk in them. At least let me wear my own shoes"

"You look stunning." Ruth wasn't sure how she had managed to keep a straight face, but she felt pleased with herself for doing so.

Leanna glared at her via her reflection, "I know what you mean, Ruth."

"The dress really complements mine, don't you think?"

At this, Leanna turned around and stormed back into the cubicle. The assistant followed her in to help her fit the dress, and consequently, Leanna took her anger out on the poor girl. *I will survive.*

"Am I allowed to tip your staff in here?" Ruth asked the manageress.

"Certainly, it's not common practice, but I'm sure the girls would appreciate it," she replied.

"Good, I want you to charge an extra hundred pounds, and it is to be given to that poor girl."

The manageress nodded her head. It wouldn't make her feel any better about the bruises she had seen, nor the abuse she had received from Leanna, but it might go some way to cheering her up. Nothing would make the shop assistant forget what she had witnessed today, and Ruth knew that she would be the gossip of the staff room, but perhaps it would be a little lessened by the joy of an unexpected hundred quid.

Leanna came stomping out of the cubicle, still in the dress, she looked like she was about to tell the whole shop, Ruth in particular, how she really felt. The harassed assistant was in tow carrying some pins in a cushion. She took a deep breath, building herself up to shout out her anger, but the manageress interrupted and spoke calmly.

"Madam looks really fashionable in that dress. Just like Naomi Campbell."

Leanna was stumped. Evidently, no one had ever made the comparison before.

"And that is no lie," Ruth added, giving her most winning smile.

Leanna was beaten. Ruth was triumphant. There were some battles that she was still strong enough to win, and she was grateful for that. Truly grateful. It gave her the impetus to carry on. 'Everything will be fine once we're married,' she thought. There would be no more Leanna, no more punishments, no more sadness. They would have the baby and life would be perfect.

"I must be going now, dear. I have to get the weight off my feet or I'll have swollen ankles for the wedding," Leanna said, obviously placated.

"Oh, … yes … Of course. I'll see you at the rehearsal. … Naomi Campbell."

Leanna's back straightened. She looked like a turquoise elephant cake topper. Ruth was about to burst with holding back the giggles.

She proceeded to the till where she paid for both dresses and the shoes with Max's card.

"Naomi Campbell is worth fifty for you too," she said to the manageress.

Again, there were two reasons for her generosity. The manageress tapped in the numbers oblivious. *I hope she has kept the dress. Max and I are still going to be married. No, no we're not, I'm going to go it alone. I will not return to that situation, never again.*

Ruth opened the door, breathing in the sweaty city air and left. As she reached the car, she heard the sound of high heels clipping quickly along the quiet street behind her, she turned expectantly, but it was not Leanna, it was the girl from the shop.

"I just wanted to say thank you, that's amazing, thank you," she said.

"I felt you deserved it," Ruth replied.

"Thank you so much," she was almost crying.

Ruth patted her arm consolingly and asked, "Is my friend still in there?"

"She left in the opposite direction to you. I best get back. But before you go..."

She reached into her pocket and produced a business card. It was black and yellow and on it was a telephone number. Ruth turned it over as she took it from her hand. On the back, was the advertisement for a domestic violence helpline.

"Just in case you fall down the stairs again," she said and smiled kindly. "You aren't the first, and you won't be the last. We have a lot of these cards, we see a lot of *accidental* bruises."

Ruth handed the card back to her. She didn't know why. It was almost as though if she took it, she would be admitting to something, some failure; something that she couldn't even begin to understand herself. What went on between Max and Ruth was different in her head, she couldn't see it as domestic violence; it was just her getting things wrong. If she didn't make so many mistakes, then it would be ok. 'Once we're married and we have the baby, it'll all be ok' she repeated to herself.

"Thank you for your concern, I really appreciate it, but honestly, I fell down the stairs, it was stupid, I just wasn't watching my step," Ruth said. *Yes, I certainly got that bit right, I was not watching my step.*

132

"Your bridesmaid told me you live in a fantastic ground floor flat," she said, and tucked the card into the pocket of Ruth's jeans.

She walked slowly back up the street to the shop, and Ruth watched her go, almost wanting to run after her and admit everything. She just couldn't get past worrying about what the girl would think of her. And what could come of it? Only another punishment. 'No one can help me, I'm alone,' she thought. Further up, Ruth spotted Leanna. She appeared to be shouting into her mobile phone and walking with that fast strut she had whenever she was mad about something. Ruth watched her, a humourless smile creeping to her lips. In her right hand was the card that the girl had given her. She was absently screwing it up into a ball, although she had no recollection of removing it from her pocket. She threw it to the ground, under the car. Sod being done for littering, there was no one around to see her anyway. She couldn't take that home with her, if it was found, it would create all sorts of issues. They were so close to the wedding now, to perfection, she didn't want to rock the boat unnecessarily. *Snap.* She got into the car and turned it around so she could drive off in the opposite direction to Leanna and her ranting. She would let her walk.

19. Max

I saw your finger move today, the little one on your left hand. It moved the tiniest bit, up and back down. The doctor said that was very promising, a fantastic sign. So well done you, now just move those eyelids open. As a treat I'm going to read again. I saw this book going for twenty pence in the hospital charity shop, and I remember you reading the whole series, waiting for the seventh and final episode. Book seven came out recently, so I've bought it for you, but it's huge, I'd lose my voice reading it aloud, so you'll just have to wake up and read it yourself, ok?

The man in black fled across the desert, and the gunslinger followed.

The desert was the apotheosis of all deserts, huge, standing to the sky for what might have been parsecs in all directions. White; blinding; waterless; without feature save for the faint, cloudy haze of the mountains which sketched themselves on the horizon and the devil-grass which brought sweet dreams, nightmares, death. An occasional tombstone sign pointed the way, for once the drifted track that cut its way through the thick crust of alkali had been a highway and coaches had followed it. The world had moved on since then. The world had emptied.

The gunslinger walked stolidly, not hurrying, not loafing.

Man, that's good reading. I have the whole set here, so I think I might read them myself while I wait. That's all I can do, isn't it? Wait. I'm sorry about last night. I guess I'm just tired. It's so hard to sit here all the time, and yet, I can't tear myself away from you. I'm in a catch 22 situation. Ha ha ha ha. And I read you that one. Should've seen it coming. Fletch and I are going for a drink tonight. I am going to leave you alone for a whole two hours. Or two and a half. He's picking me up at eight-thirty and I'll be back at about eleven-thirty. Or maybe before that. He brought in some Sudoku books and said I should challenge my brain. Talking to you for hours on end isn't really a challenge. It's all the rage apparently. Looks crap to me, but I will try, he had my best interests at heart I guess. I'll leave some for you to do as you're getting better. You can be challenged. It'll be nice to have a break, won't it? Even if it's only a couple of hours. Better than nothing. He's done the moving by the way. But he didn't unpack any boxes with your name on because he didn't think you'd like that much. I would have thought you'd be grateful. I guess it'll give us something to do when we go home anyway.

I keep thinking of the time you left me. I was so scared. I knew you knew that I'd slept with Leanna. I stayed up all night listening to your favourite two albums, the only two you own, over and over again. When you came home, I said all the things that you wanted to hear, but I was lying Ruth. I never ended it with Leanna. I never have. That's why she came here a few nights ago. I tried to end it then. She's stopped calling me now. It's over now. I promise it's over. I'm not going to tell Fletch though. I can't destroy two people. One was bad enough.

I spoilt you rotten after that night when you found out about me and Leanna. I didn't know how else I could make you stay. But I knew that you liked things. Material things. So I bought stuff, flowers, that teddy. It was never going to make it right though was it. I was so angry with you for allowing me to cheat. But I should have been angry at myself. Now I just feel guilty.

20. Ruth

Max was already there when Ruth arrived home. He was standing in the doorway as though he had been waiting for her. His face was clouded with thunder. Ruth spent longer than necessary packing up her bag in the car, composing herself. She wished she had something on her to protect her stomach, although she didn't think even he would hit her there now. It was too distended, too clearly defined as containing another life. *I was so hopeful, so misguided. I really, really, can never make those same mistakes again. I've never really been on my own, and I won't be alone again. I'll have my baby. I don't need anyone else.*

Ruth also couldn't believe he would have the audacity to have a go at her about Leanna and her dress. That was all she could think it was about. She had done nothing else to rile him. She planned her retorts as she randomly took stuff from her bag and put it back in again. 'You had the affair with her.' 'What, afraid your shag-piece will look bad?' 'She's just exaggerating to cause an argument.' 'Why were you even talking to her?' Ruth smirked at the last one and straightened up to remove the keys from the ignition. She jumped about a foot in the air. Max was standing silently staring in at her through the driver's side window. Instantly, she knew that she wouldn't say anything. He looked more terrifying than she had ever seen him before.

Ruth looked at him, trying to be puzzled by his behaviour, trying to convey some kind of innocence. Her face screwed up comically, trying to show that she didn't understand. She was grasping at some kind of vulnerability that would shield her from his hands. 'Why didn't he just tap on the window to get my attention?' she thought. He glared back at her, anger coursing through his features. She unlocked the door and stepped out of the car. She had to face him at some point, there wasn't enough petrol to drive very far and she had pretty much maxed out his credit card.

"Hi honey, did you have a good day?" She stood on tiptoes to kiss him. He didn't respond.

"Ok, obviously not."

She turned in a tight circle so that she could lock the door, he was that close to her, she couldn't move properly. He grabbed her by her elbow and marched her back to the flat. He was dragging her along, her trainers, a necessity for her currently bloated pregnancy feet, scuffed along the pavement. She couldn't keep up. His fingernails dug into her flesh and hurt her, making her eyes water, but there was no point in telling him that. She knew that he was beyond reason. There was nothing she could say or do to stave off the inevitable. She just hoped the baby would survive. She was frightened, her teeth chattered as he dragged her along. *No caesarean, I'm too frightened.* She was beyond frightened, she was absolutely, abjectly, terrified. She didn't even think she knew a word that could accommodate the extent of her fear. He was bare foot. For some reason, this sight twisted her stomach into one gigantic knot.

He hauled her into the hall and slammed the door behind them; it shook in the frame. He hurled her into the lounge. She tripped on the rug and fell, she just caught herself to protect her bump at the last second. She landed on her back on the sofa. She was trembling. *Snap.* She could feel sweat on her freshly waxed upper lip, it itched. He stared down at her, breathing hard. She met his eyes, but her look was less intimidating, more pleading. She was so scared, he had never been like this before. He had been bad, but nothing, *nothing* like this.

"I had a call from Leanna today."

"Oh?" she whispered.

'If this is about her' she thought, 'If this is anything about her, I'll never forgive him. I'll walk, I really will.' She couldn't carry on if he chose her feelings over Ruth's. *If only I'd stuck to that conviction. If only I hadn't destroyed that card.*

137

"Yeah, she said you've picked out the worst dress there is for her to wear."

"So that's why you're so angry, afraid you're bit of stuff won't look good at your wedding? Well, she was exaggerating anyway. The dress could be much worse."

She didn't know why she had just said that, her mouth didn't feel like it was her own and her brain was suddenly spinning with the implications of that one comment. It was like lighting the touch paper of a TNT bomb, only unlike in the cartoons, they wouldn't all walk away without a mark on them. She felt sick. 'Perhaps, this will be the end. Perhaps I've pushed him too far,' she thought.

"No, that's not why I'm angry."

Ruth watched his face move like a broiling sea.

"Here I am. The mug, the fool. All this time, I've been feeling guilty for Leanna, feeling that I've let you down. But no, I was wrong."

Confusion lit up her mind blocking all other thoughts out. She couldn't seem to get her overwrought mind around the concept of him feeling guilty, never mind him mentioning the forbidden subject. She opened her mouth and then closed it, she didn't know what to say. She opened it again, this time, words formed into sentences ready to come out.

"What are you talking about? I don't understand."

He picked up a cushion and threw it at her, into her face. It was plush and soft, but the force and the angle still made it hurt as it landed on the bridge of her nose. She removed the cushion and put her left hand to her nostrils, she pulled it away and a sliver of blood lingered on her fingers. *Snap.* She looked back at him, her mouth hung open in disbelief.

"You slag," he said and walked out of the room and into the kitchen.

She stood up shakily and followed him. *I should have run away. Why is it that the victim falls for the predator? What is the attraction, the ignorance, the stupidness that allows the predator*

138

such ease in getting to his prey? He was at the counter pouring a large portion of scotch into a glass. *Please let me live, I'll be good.*

Max slowly revolved on the spot and watched her over the rim of his glass. He took a large gulp. Ruth could feel the blood as it dripped over my lip; she could taste the rustiness as it crept into her mouth. She felt overwhelmingly sick, but it would be worse if she tried to hide in the bathroom. The door between them would fuel his anger.

"You know what you've done to deserve this."

"No, I'm afraid I don't Max, in fact, I think you've completely lost it."

He stepped towards her, the glass raised in his hand, and she wondered if he was going to brain her with it. She didn't think so though. She thought he was in control, to a certain extent. She didn't think he would hit her anywhere that people would see when she was in her wedding dress. She knew she was right when his fist landed on her ribs on her left side. It was not as bad as it could have been, he was left handed and punched with his right as the left held the glass. His right was weaker, not much, but a bit. She still doubled over in pain. It still hurt.

"You slept with Fletch."

Each word was punctuated by another blow. In his left hand, the scotch didn't even spill. His right hand did the damage, uninterested in where he landed it, just caring that it connected with her flesh. He struck her upper arm, her chest, her ribs. Ruth heard a crack, and thought that possibly, one of her already overstretched ribs, expanded to accommodate her child, had snapped. *Snap.*
Shock ran from her head to her toes, numbing her extremities. Leanna. If only the woman had known what she had done to Ruth. Leanna's ignorance was her bliss and Ruth's pain. Ruth hoped that she found out though, before he did it to her too. As his punches rained down, Ruth was thinking of Leanna's safety, not her own. *Ever the loving, generous character. I admit it, part of it was my fault. I let people walk all over me. I'm not saying I deserved it, not*

139

as such, what I'm saying is that I never cared for myself as much as I did for other people, and I suffered because of that. Now, I need to put me, me and my baby, first. I need to stop with the worrying about other people, let them make their own lives, their own decisions, and I will now make mine.

"And who told you that Max? Was it your poor, pissed-off ex-lover?" Ruth gasped as air rattled into her winded lungs. Each breath almost made her scream in pain.

His eyes narrowed, "Yes." She was home free, well, in less danger at least.

"And you never thought she was lying? You never thought to ask me? You just assumed that because you think so little of me that you cheat on me that I would be the same, I would cheat on you? I would go off and shag your best mate in revenge? Never occurred to you to talk to me?"

Dark patches bloomed in front of her eyes, they were tinged with rainbows, a sure sign that at any moment, she would faint. She had fainted before, a few years previously. He just continued to kick her until he had become bored. She knew that was what happened because he had told her afterwards, and, to confirm his story, she had a boot print on her back, and another on her shoulder. She couldn't faint when he was in this condition. She wouldn't survive, and neither would her bump. She bit down on her lip until she had drawn blood. It was another pain on top of all the others, but this was one she could control, one that she had created, and it brought her back to full consciousness.

"Leanna said Fletch had told her all about it," he said.

"And did you ask Fletch?"

"Yes, and he laughed at me. He said Leanna was dreaming." His face betrayed how much Fletch laughing had hurt him, a clue as to why he was so exceptionally angry. He hated to lose face in front of his friends, he hated for them to laugh at him, unless he intended it.

"And you didn't believe him."

"No." Ruth could almost hear him finishing the sentence petulantly with, 'he laughed at me.' It was on his mind, it was almost all he could think about. She knew him so well. In some ways, he was in fact quite predictable.

"Right. Well, for your information, I have never cheated on you." *I lied. I think that was the worst moment. I lied to stay safe when I should've just walked. Snap. But what else could I do? If I'd told him the truth, he would've killed me there and then. If I'd walked, he was in the frame of mind that would've led him to follow me, and, most probably, kill me then.*

She backed slowly away from him, arms outstretched in front of her, like she was training a wild tiger. She could taste the metallic flavour of her blood as more of it trickled over her lip and into my mouth. Some from her nose, some from her torn lip. It was the blood from her lip that gave her the strength to keep going. When she reached the door, she retreated down the corridor into the relative safety of the locked bathroom. She was constantly tense as she shuffled down the hallway, waiting for him to round the corner. She continued to walk backwards so that she could see him coming if he did. But she didn't run. If she ran, it would be like playing chase in the playground, only this game would have dire consequences.

She sat on the lid of the toilet and leaned over into the sink, she mopped her face up with the flannel. When the blood stopped, she burst into tears and cried for what felt like forever. She lifted her t-shirt and could see the bruise that was forming across the top of her stomach, it started at the side, and then spread over the shell in which her baby resided. The baby wasn't moving. She sat silently, rubbing her bump gently, delicately, waiting for some sign that all would be well. Eventually, there was a small movement, tiny, but enough to appease her. She started to cry again, but this time, it was with relief. Her baby seemed fine. As if in response to that, it kicked her very gently, she could see the movement, but barely felt it, as she was aching and hurting so much.

141

Her joy at this moment, at what she saw as a true love event; was interrupted by Max knocking the door. The sound seemed loud, deafening almost, although it wasn't, he was being temperate, it was time for him to show his sorrow and calmness. They had been there before, and they both knew it. They had rituals.

"I know I keep on saying it, but I'm sorry Ruth. I guess I wanted justification for my own behaviour. Open the door, let me look at your nose."

She sat on the toilet and debated on whether to let him in or not. She was in agony. Her nose hurt, her stomach was doing summersaults, her heart felt as if it had been ripped to shreds. She couldn't take anymore. *Snap.* She couldn't live like this. She opened the door. Max came in and cupped her face carefully in his hands, turning it to the light so he could see the damage more clearly. *It had been a long time coming. I know that now. Now I can reflect.*

"The bleeding has stopped. I don't think it's broken."

He gently kissed the tip of her nose, brushed it with his lips. He didn't ask about the baby. He didn't ask about the point where his spite connected agonisingly with my ribs.

"I love you Ruth, I really do."

"No you don't." There was truth in that, she could feel it. She knew he didn't love her, but yet, she so desperately needed him to love her. She needed him to tell her that she was wrong. She needed him to make everything right again like he always did.

"I do love you, I love you more than anyone or anything, and that is why I get so angry," he said, his hands caressed her cheeks, wiped away her tears. *So many pissing bloody excuses! From me, but more so from him. I will not take it anymore. This stops.*

Their words reverberated around her skull, never sinking in or staying put. They bounced back and forth, damaging the interior of her mind. He put his arm around her and led her to the living room. He guided her to the chair in front of the television and returned to the kitchen. She could hear him going through the

142

drawers, searching out the menus so he could order a take away. She wasn't hungry though. She never wanted to eat again. She stared at the television without seeing the images, or hearing the voices. *If only I'd known how that would really feel, I might not have done what I did.*

Her mind reeled with the repercussions the evening's events. If she had told him the truth, what then? She had a flashback, a split second image, from her childhood, of seeing her mother unconscious on the kitchen floor. Her nose broken, her eyes bruised and puffed up, the only movement coming from the damaged shuddering made by each breath she took. Ruth didn't want to end up like that. She didn't want to be in the same place her Mam had been. She was going to have to do something about it. She needed to think. *Snap. And then I forgot.*

21. Little Ruth

For the next few days, Ruth barely spoke to anyone, not even Mam. She wouldn't ride her bike or play with her Barbies, she would only read her book. Mam spoke to her teacher at school and on the Friday, she even took her to the doctor. But all they said was that Ruth was sad at the loss of Father. On Saturday morning, she came down for breakfast, her book in her hand and didn't even say good morning to Mam. *More guilt, more things I wish I could make amends for, but it's too late.* She had dressed herself and was wearing a mish-mash of clothes. She had on a blue jumper with a green skirt, a yellow necklace and pink wellie boots. She sat at the table and put her book by her plate. Mam had cooked her a wonderful breakfast of bacon and eggs. She placed it down in front of Ruth, who just stared at it.

"Come on darling, I know you're sad, but you must eat," Mam said.

Ruth didn't reply, she fiddled with the corner of the cover of her book and continued to stare at her plate.

"Daddy does love you, but he doesn't love Mummy anymore, so he can't live with us. He will visit you soon."

Ruth looked up at Mam, shocked out of her self-enforced Coventry. This news had rocked her to the very core, and now, she knew the reason why Father had gone.

"I hate you! You made my Daddy go away!" she screamed. *It wasn't her, why couldn't I see that? Why did I have to make everything so much harder for her? He was in the wrong, not Mam, just like Max is in the wrong, not me.*

She grabbed her book and leapt from the table, she ran out of the kitchen through the hall and out of the front door. Mam came after her, but she wasn't quite quick enough. Ruth ran across the road and through the car park. She sprinted past the people in the allotments, the wind whipping her hair and stinging her cheeks until they were red. She ran all the way until the end of the rows where

144

there was just grass and a few trees. She aimed for the tallest fir, stuffed her book into the waist band of her skirt and began to climb.

She sat in the top most branch the whole day, she heard Mam calling her name but she would not go back. By the time the sun started to go down, Ruth was very cold, very hungry and was feeling bad about what she had said to Mam. She was still angry at her, but she really did love her. Maybe if she told Mam that she had to make Father love her again then Mam would make an effort. Some of the other Mothers wore lipstick and things in their hair, if Mam did that, then she was sure Father would return. *I don't believe that I seriously wanted him back. I wanted someone, him, but not him, another Father, one that had all the good things and none of the bad.* Ruth started to climb down the branches and was almost ready to jump the last few feet, two strong hands reached around her waist and pulled her down.

A gruff, kindly voice said, "Now then lassy, your Mam's worried about you, let's get you home."

The strange man smelled familiar and comfortable and he carried her in his solid arms all the way to her front door where he rang the bell. Ruth had rested her head in the hollow of his shoulder and sucked her thumb all the way home and hadn't looked at him. As the bell rang, she lifted her head and recognised him as the nice man who lived next door. He smiled at her and ruffled her hair as Mam opened the door. His wife was standing behind her. She smiled at Ruth and put her hand on Mam's arm.

"There she is Val, told you there was no need to worry yourself." said the lady. The man passed Ruth over to Mam's open arms. She was crying and clutched at Ruth as if she would never let her go again. The lady and the man came into the kitchen with Ruth and Mam.

"Now then Bob, go and get us all some fish and chips from up the road and I'll put the kettle on." The lady busied herself around the kitchen, cleaning up the things from the uneaten breakfast that had sat on the table all day long. She made Mam a strong cup of

145

tea. Mam just sat at the table, Ruth in her arms, crying and rocking backwards and forwards.

"You're best shot of him Val," she said. "How long did you think you could live like that? Ruth will understand one day."

"I know," said Mam. "It's just so hard, he won't give me any money and I don't have a job. He calls so late at night that I can't wake Ruth." Mam started to cry again and the rest of her words became unintelligible.

"Hush dear, hush," said the lady, then she took Ruth away from Mam to get her into her nightie and her dressing gown before tea. When they returned Bob was back and Mam was looking much better. The radio was on in the kitchen and there were four lots of fish and chips set out in the paper on the table. Ruth sat down in her seat and looked at Mam, unsure as to whether or not it was alright to start eating yet. She wasn't used to having people in for tea. It had always been better for them to keep themselves to themselves. She nodded at Ruth, so she dug in. She hadn't eaten properly for nearly a week and was desperately hungry. *I was like that with Max too, when things were bad. It worries me now, what if my baby's too small because I didn't eat enough? What if I've made my baby ill?*

"I'm sorry, I haven't introduced you!" said Mam. "This is Uncle Bob and Aunty Jean from next door. They helped me look for you."

"My name is Ruth," she said to Aunty Jean and Uncle Bob, trying to prove that she wasn't always naughty.

After tea was over, Uncle Bob took out a pipe and started to smoke it. He made great puffs of chalky looking smoke appear from the end of the pipe and the corners of his mouth at the same time. Ruth stared at him for a few minutes before deciding that he seemed not only nice, but interesting too. Mam and Aunty Jean were talking grown-up things, so Ruth slipped from her chair and crawled under the table. She scrambled up onto Uncle Bob's lap using his jumper to haul herself over his long legs. He put his arm around her and

146

carried on smoking the sweet smelling pipe as he hummed a soft, delicate tune in her ear.

She woke up the next morning feeling a lot better and went downstairs to tell Mam. She wasn't in the kitchen where she would normally be of a morning. The kitchen looked as though it had been ransacked. There was paper everywhere, it smothered the table, it had spilled on to the floor and was covering the worktops on the units. Ruth picked up a piece of the paper near her foot. In bold letters at the top it said Gas, she picked up another and this said Bank Statement. Ruth put the papers back on the floor and walked into the living room. Mam was asleep on the settee with the previous day's newspaper over her eyes. *Sometimes, money is necessary. We were broke, properly skint in the true sense of the word, and all because of my Father and his new bit of stuff. He was so busy splashing out on her, making her feel like he was the best thing since sliced bread, that he had forgotten about us and we suffered.*

Ruth went back into the kitchen and climbed on a chair to fill the kettle so that it was half empty, she had learnt from her previous tea-making exploits. She pulled a chair across to the cupboard with the mugs and teabags in. She put a teabag in one of the nice mugs with poppies on it and climbed back down. She took the mug to the kettle and climbed up on the chair again to fill the mug with hot water. She got a teaspoon and stirred the tea. She took the black tea, the way Mam liked it, back into the living room. She put it on the coffee table and gently shook Mam awake. *I was always so desperate to be perfect, to get things right, so that I could have a Mother and Father in my life. I loved Mam, I really did, but she wasn't coping, and I just didn't know what to do about it.*

"I made you tea and I didn't blow anything up." she said as Mam opened her eyes.

Mam sat up and Ruth passed her the tea. Mam looked at her and gave her a stunning smile. Ruth was surprised by how happy she looked, surprised and confused, it wasn't something she had ever seen before.

"You are such a clever girl," she said, "Now, while I have your full attention, I need to tell you something important."

Deep pain swilled around Ruth's stomach. Her thoughts raced through her head and fear that Mam was leaving too engulfed her. She might not look sad like Father had, but that really didn't mean anything. She just didn't trust anyone anymore, not really. *And if I'm honest, completely honest, I haven't since.*

"Are you feeling alright darling? You've gone ever so pale." Mam said.

"I'm ok," Ruth replied.

"Well then, my news is that we are going to have to get rid of some things until Mummy gets a job. Once Mummy is working, you might have to stay with Aunty Jean and Uncle Bob sometimes after school. They said they'd love to have you and Aunty Jean will teach you how to make cakes and Uncle Bob says he'll help you with your homework."

"Will my toys have to go?" asked Ruth.

"No, not your toys, but things like the television and the big dressers."

Ruth thought about it and decided that as long as she could still borrow books from school like *The Magic Faraway Tree* then she wouldn't really miss the television. Ruth and Mam spent the day together deciding what could be sold and what couldn't. Mam wrote the list because Ruth wrote slowly. By the evening they had listed everything they owned and rented and what they would be returning or selling in the week.

That night, Father called. He wouldn't speak to Mam, but he spent a long time on the phone talking to Ruth.

"Please come home now," she said.

"I can't, I don't love your Mummy anymore Princess."

"I promise she'll be a better Mummy now, and then you won't have to fight and you can live at home," Ruth replied

148

Father sighed and said, "I can't Ruth, I love you, just not Mummy and it's too hard now."

Ruth still didn't understand why he couldn't come home. She told him that she was reading really big children's' books at school and that they were selling things in the house because he was away. He asked to speak to Mam and so she handed the phone over, but stood next to it so she could hear what was being said.

"Rick, I have to keep the roof over our heads. I haven't a job and you're only paying the school fees. She still needs clothes, food and things for school and there's the mortgage and the bills, I have to," Mam said.

Ruth could hear Father shouting back in return but not his words.

"You left *us* Rick, we are just coping with the aftermath." And then she slammed the handset back into its cradle, making the little bell jingle.

Each day, Ruth came home and something else had gone. The television; the big mahogany units; the three-piece suite; the fish tank in the kitchen with its bright shiny fish. One day, Mam met her at school with her bike and told Ruth that she'd sold the car so they would be walking home, but Ruth could ride her bike. *I hated that bike, I really hated it, it was just Him in purple shiny paint.* Ruth glared at Mam and refused to get on the bike. She could understand that a television wasn't a necessity, but not how the car could be given up.

Mam dragged her kicking and screaming all the way home, carrying the bike in her other hand. They got to the front gate and Uncle Bob was in his garden next door. He came over to the hedge.

"Give her here Valerie," he said.

He picked Ruth up and she still struggled and kicked and shouted. He carried her into the back garden and showed her the tadpoles in the pond.

"Here missy," he said, "Now what's all the fuss about?"

149

"Mam sold the car and made me walk home from school, no one else has to walk home from school, I want my Daddy back," Ruth replied, snot and tears streaming down her face.

Uncle Bob took a handkerchief from his pocket and cleaned her up. He carried her into the kitchen and gave her a biscuit and a glass of lemonade. Auntie Jean came in and looked from Uncle Bob to Ruth and back again.

"I've just seen your Mum," she said, "And I've invited her over for a special dinner tonight. Are you going to help me cook something special for her?"

Ruth nodded and said, "Can it be pizza?"

"That sounds quite nice, but what about spaghetti bolognaise? I bet she'd love that."

Ruth agreed. She knew she'd been naughty, but she knew Mam would forgive her, just like she'd always forgiven Father when he'd been naughty. *I will learn, I can learn. I'm not stupid. Mam learnt. Almost.*

22. Ruth

It was the right thing to do at the time. Ruth spent the next week in a daze. She watched Max at a distance as he attended to her every whim. All she wanted to do though was sleep. She went to bed early and woke up late and then in the afternoons, she napped. She dreamed inconsequential dreams. Max married Leanna in a beautiful ceremony. Ruth was there, but as a child, and she was the bridesmaid in a black dress. She saw her mother; she came to sit with her.

"You can't carry on like this," Mam said as she reclined in the armchair next to the television.

Ruth was torn between Ricki Lake and answering her. Mam was pale and was wearing her favourite dress. The lime green one with big padded shoulders. Her huge, house brick sized mobile phone was in her lap. It didn't ring, which Ruth found strange. It never used to stop when she was a teenager. Mam had been an invaluable addition to the office, according to her boss that Ruth had met one year at the Christmas do. He had seemed to truly like Mam, and appreciate her. She was happy then.

"You have to make your escape. You *can* make it on your own. I'll be with you."

"You won't," Ruth replied, "You left me once, you'll do it again." *Why didn't Max notice?*

Ruth was fascinated by the way her Mam's lips moved. It was as if they were always pursed in anger or disapproval, and her words had to be scrunched out between them in spurts. That was something that had come with the job. When Ruth had been small, Mam's lips had been plump and kind. *I think it was all imagined, but even so, it was real. She was so disappointed, so upset that I was in her situation, that I had made the same mistakes. I just wanted to say sorry to her, to tell her everything about how I felt, about how I'd treated her in those first years after He'd left, but all I could do was be petulant. Ever the child.* Her Mam always left

151

when Max came in the room. Ruth never saw her go, but then she never saw her arrive either. She was just there and then not there. Ruth's hair was tangled. *And now I have no hair, happy?* She watched television while she was awake, seeing but not seeing it. She often slept on the sofa because the effort involved in getting up and going to the bedroom was far too great to bother with. She didn't eat; she didn't see the need to.

Max had finally stopped hitting her. After the blood, after the bruises, he stopped. He treated her with kid gloves. If she wanted an orange, all she needed to do was put one foot on the floor, and he was there, asking her what she wanted, running to get it. He would peel the orange and put the segments on a plate so that she didn't even have to separate them out. *I should have been scared, but I was lost instead.*

Mam came to visit on one particular day. She sat in the chair opposite Ruth and smiled. Ruth could see how much she loved her, and it made her very bones ache.

"I wish you'd learnt from my mistakes," Mam said.

"So do I," she replied, and she meant it this time, at that moment in time.

"He wasn't all bad, and neither is your Max, but there are some things that just cannot be changed. Sometimes, there is something not right in a person that runs too deep for it to ever be corrected."

"I think you're right."

Ruth couldn't take her eyes from her Mam. She wanted to reach out and touch her, to creep into her arms and hug her, but Ruth knew that if she moved, if she tried, then Mam would disappear again. She wanted to return to those few years, that short period of time, when it was just them, her and her Mam and no one else. Ruth and Mam making ends meet. She smiled at the memory of that time. Her Mam returned her smile.

"It was good then, wasn't it?" Mam asked.

"Best years of my life."

"Mine too," she said. "But we knew in our hearts it wouldn't go on forever. I hadn't learnt my lesson. I needed one more. You should've learnt then Ruth. I kept on at you to be careful."

She was right, she had always been right. Ruth looked down at her ragged finger nails. She had chewed them until there was no edge left, and when she looked up again, Mam had gone. She left behind her an emptiness that nothing could fill. *I think I've learnt to accept this now, or at least, I will be able to accept it once I move on. Once I escape. Once I've learnt my lesson. I have learnt my lesson.*

Max came into the room, he looked at her bloated figure and smiles. No more spiteful comments about how she looked. He was on best behaviour. She wondered vaguely if he noticed the change in her, Ruth noticed it. She wondered if he had noticed that Ruth had cracked.

"Who were you talking to?" he asked.

"Myself," Ruth replied. She could see no point in wasting the truth on him. It would bypass go and not collect two hundred pounds.

"Mad people talk to themselves," he said, and chuckled, he ruffled her hair.

She could still hear him laughing and muttering in the kitchen. Ruth closed her eyes and went to sleep.

When she woke up, it was dark. He had put the spare blanket over her on the sofa, but she liked to think that it was Mam who had done it. It was the early hours of the morning, three, maybe four. She could hear Max snoring from the bedroom, it was a soothing sound. She liked him best these days when he was asleep. She suddenly realised that Mam was back, hidden in the shadows.

"Why don't you just leave?" Mam asked. "He's asleep, you could be far away by the morning. You have money, you'll be fine."

"No Mam, he's changed, honestly. He hasn't hit me in ages, no comments, nothing. He's lovely again."

"He's not pumpkin, he's the same."

153

"Mam, you don't know him like I do. I can tell."

Mam sighed and shook her head. Ruth could see the disappointment in her eyes. Ruth wished she could see her grow old. She wished she could watch wrinkles form on her face and her eyes crinkle. That would never happen, if Ruth knew nothing else, she knew that. It made her sad. She wondered if the gnawing inside her was due to Mam being there, or because she was hungry. She didn't know when she had last eaten.

"Mam, can you do me a cuppa while I have a shower?" Ruth asked, but it was too late. She had gone.

Ruth tiptoed into the bedroom and took clean clothes from the wardrobe. Max didn't even stir. Mam had been right, she could have just left. He would never know, until the morning, anyway. She entered the bathroom and went through the motions that she had gone through every day of her adult life. Teeth, pee, shower. She got dressed in clean jogging bottoms and a clean t-shirt. All sense of style was long gone. It had been the first of her senses to fail her. She went into the kitchen and made some tea and toast. She could still hear Max snoring. The smell of the browning bread made her stomach growl in anticipation. Her baby began to shift. She put two more slices in before she had even begun to butter the first round.

Eventually, her needs satisfied, she returned to the sofa. She was not tired at all. It was odd, but once Max was sleeping, she felt very much awake. Perhaps it was her body giving her a hint about what she should do next, she thought. *If only I'd listened to that body. The whole world would be different right now.* She turned on the television and watched overly made-up women try to sell cheap costume jewellery at a huge mark-up. They pretended it was a bargain. Mam wouldn't come back now. It was too close to Max getting up. Just as this thought crossed her mind, she heard Max getting out of bed. The springs creaked ominously. She could tell he was trying to be quiet so that he didn't wake her.

He came into the lounge dressed for work. She smiled, distantly pleased that he was heading into the office, rather than

154

hanging around watching over her. Perhaps today would be her chance.

"Good morning gorgeous," he said.

She turned her beaming face towards him, trying to make it look like she meant it.

"I have to go into the office this morning, but I'll back later, about lunchtime, I'll bring you something nice to eat."

The smile seemed plastered to her face as though it had been painted on with clown makeup. She nodded her head and waited for him to leave. Impatiently. She would do it today. He bent down and kissed her nose and then, finally, he left.

As soon as he was out of the door, she ran to the bedroom. She pulled out a medium sized suitcase from the selection under the bed. She half filled it with pregnancy wear, and half with her normal clothes. Instead of packing by outfit like she normally would, she just grabbed handfuls of clothes and threw them in. She didn't know how long she would need the pregnancy stuff for, so the reserve clothes were in preparation for the inevitable. *If only, if only.* She chucked in shoes, sensible, and nice ones, the first pairs that came to hand. She remembered underwear just before she shut the case. She threw in as many as would fit, grabbing them from the drawer, not caring any more. She swiped all the potions and lotions from the top of the dresser into the case. Ruth zipped it up, put on her trainers, and headed for the door. She collected her coat on the way through the hall.

She flung open the front door, ready to embrace freedom, and he was stood there. A snide smile sat on his lips.

"I knew you were faking it. All this perfect behaviour has been to lull me into a false sense of security, so that you could leave me. Stupid bitch."

He pushed her back into the hallway, she almost tripped over the suitcase, but he saved her, by grabbing a fistful of her t-shirt and using it to yank her upright. He slammed the door behind him.

155

He had never, ever beaten me as badly as he did that night. I was completely unconscious. But he got what he wanted. He reminded me of why I was scared of him, why I couldn't leave him. Why I shouldn't leave him. It was weeks before I could walk properly. The next thing I consciously knew, even though I had only been out for a few days, was that the wedding was upon us. Mam had stopped visiting by then. I think I imagined her coming to give me the impetus to leave, but that once I'd given in, I had no reason to imagine her anymore. I missed her though.

23. Ruth

Leanna and Bethany arrived the night before the wedding. Max left to stay with Fletcher. He kissed Ruth's lips before he left. She didn't reciprocate, she didn't speak. She was beyond talking now. Her body was still bruised, she was still in pain every time she moved. Leanna and Bethany didn't notice, they were having fun, painting each other's toenails. It was like she was watching a movie of a slumber party. In three dimensional glory. She could even reach out and touch the characters if she really wanted to. Her hand snaked towards Leanna's shoulder before she realised what she was doing and snatched it back again.

Leanna and Bethany had brought *Muriel's Wedding* with them. As if Ruth wanted to watch rubbish like that. They sat either side of her on the sofa laughing and singing along to the Abba songs. Ruth couldn't see the humour. It was Muriel that did it. She's like Ruth at first, no self-esteem, no love at home, well, her Mother tries. Ruth's loved her. Properly. The one and only time anyone had loved her. The difference between Ruth and Muriel is that Muriel gets a happy ending. Ruth knew she wouldn't have a happy ending. That was not in her movie. *It is. I will have a happy ending.*

The movie began to depress her, so she stared at her fingernails and picked at them until there was nothing left to pick at. *How did no one save me?* She stood up and left to go to bed, choosing the best option of a bad lot. It was nine o'clock, which was plenty late enough for Ruth. She didn't get undressed before she climbed beneath the quilt. She loved her quilt. Her body smelt foul. She couldn't remember the last time she had a shower. She pulled the quilt right up to her chin to suffocate the aroma. She was cocooned in her own flesh. *My own mind.* She just couldn't bear to look at herself in the mirror, and the bathroom had lots of mirrors. It hurt to look.

She listened to Leanna and Bethany talk about her in the living room. She caught snippets of what they were saying. Enough to know that they seemed to be worried about her, however superficially. Not enough to figure out if they were going to try and help. Ruth felt as though she should get naked and go back into the room, let them really understand how wonderful Max was, let them experience it for themselves. She smirked at the thought. But no, she was too worried that he would then go for them too. She might not like them very much, but nobody deserved that. *I am nobody. I didn't deserve it either.*

Mam sat on the end of Ruth's bed. She hadn't seen her arrive, but suddenly she was there. Ruth could even feel the weight of her body next to her feet. She was surprised to see her. It had been a while since Mam was last around. *I'd forgotten about this visit. I forgot that she never gave up. There was another visit too, but that was me.* Ruth felt a warmth spread through her, an empty happiness that she always had in Mam's presence.

"Tell them pumpkin," she said. "Go in there and tell them."

"I can't Mam, I can't. He'll kill us all."

"He can't hurt them, they're protected. And once you tell them, then you'll be safe too."

"I'll never be safe Mam. I know that as well as you do."

She patted Ruth's leg, Ruth felt her hand as she watched it. She smiled at Ruth, her eyes brimming with tears. Ruth's follow suit, and as she tried to blink them away, Mam disappeared. Life was so hard, but she had to do the best she could with what she had.

157

What she had was a man that said he loved her. A lot. And she was carrying his child, and they were going to get married. She closed her eyes and hoped that the girls wouldn't come in. She could feel the tears seeping under her eyelashes, and imagined them running their course, across her face, into the pillow, never to be seen again.

How I survived that last twenty-four hours, I'll never know, and to be honest, I almost didn't. But watch me now. If I focus really hard, I can feel my toes. I can feel my toe nails pressing into the sheet that covers me. I can get better, and when I do, I will make my life better. Max can leave

24. Little Ruth

There are two distinct visits I remember, the first when I was eight or so, the second when I was twelve or thirteen. I know there were others, but it was these two that stuck in my mind, these two that I should've learnt from. I've never learnt, but I have now. It has just taken more time than expected.

Ruth sat on the bottom stair in her very best outfit. She was wearing a red pleated skirt with a red and green tartan blouse. It had an itchy white collar with a lace trim. Ruth kept fiddling with it, much to Mam's annoyance.

"Stop it, you'll crease it, you need to look tidy," Mam said.

Ruth didn't reply, but did fold her hands in her lap. Mam seemed more worried than she was. She'd never really spent time alone with Father, this would be a first. She was nervous, but excited. Very excited. She missed him still. She loved him as though he'd never done all the bad things. In her heart, she was struggling with her emotions, because in her heart, she knew he was a bad man, but he was still her Father.

The reason she was sat on the bottom stair and the reason Mam was still bustling around was that he was late. Ruth had got up early, was ready to go an hour before he was due, she hadn't wanted to anger him by being late. Mam had approved of this and had smiled while she was cleaning. The entire house looked like a fairy had come along and sprinkled it with sparkles. Now, however, he was almost an hour late, which meant Ruth had sat on the bottom stair for two hours. Her bum was numb. *Always waiting, always.*

Each time a car pulled up, or even just drove past, Mam ran to the nearest window and peeked around the net curtains. Finally, it was the right car.

"He's here love, off you go, have a good day."

Mam let Ruth out the front door. Ruth turned to kiss her goodbye, but couldn't do it. It felt as though every tear running down her Mam's face was tearing at her heart. She was scared,

159

terrified even, that she wouldn't see her Mam again, although she knew that there were court laws that said that wouldn't happen. *There were many times like that, but this was the one I never forgot, the one that stands alone, rather than being a part of a montage.*

"I'll be back soon Mam, chocolate for tea, yeah?"

Mam couldn't say anything. She closed the door, and Ruth turned away and began the longest walk of her life. The twelve foot shuffle down the path to the front gate and the waiting car. As she got closer, she realised that there was someone already sat in the passenger seat. The tall Dolly Parton replica stepped from the car. She glared at Ruth.

"Your Dad said you're to sit in the front," she snarled.

Ruth only knew one swear word, it was the all encompassing 'bugger'. In her mind, she could hear her Mam saying, 'Bugger this for a game of soldiers.' Although Ruth wasn't entirely sure what the line meant, she felt it appropriate to this situation. Whoever this woman was, she clearly didn't like Ruth, and she didn't even know her. Ruth on the other hand, found her quite interesting, in the way any life-size Barbie doll would be interesting to a little girl. *I wanted to poke her leg or her arm to see if she was made of plastic.*

Ruth smiled, and climbed into the passenger seat. Father leant across and kissed her on the cheek, but missed, as Ruth jumped when the woman slammed the door.

"Stupid cow," he muttered and started the car engine.

For a split second, Ruth thought he would drive off without the woman, but she scrambled into the back of the car and closed the door just as he was pulling away from the curb. *The silence that ensued was so painful. Excruciating.* Ruth just wanted to go home to Mam and have crumpets and tea. Mam had told her that she was a big girl now, she was in junior school and everything, and so she should be brave and spend the day with Father. It wouldn't kill her. Ruth was beginning to think that maybe Mam had that last bit wrong as the car sped along the motorway, the silence seemingly endless.

After what felt like a lifetime, they pulled into a car park, and once the engine had stopped and all that could be heard was the tick as it cooled, Father spoke.

"Ruth, this is Cheryl, she's going to be your new Mam."

"It's *Cheryl*, not *Sheryl*. Nice to meet you Ruth." *She was a brave woman, it was never destined to last. I wish I'd realised that at the time and then I might have had a better humour during the day. Then I wouldn't have spent every second fearing that I would never see Mam again.*

Ruth thought she was going to be sick. New Mam? What was he on about? She had a Mam, *her* Mam. She didn't need another one.

"Cheryl and me are getting a house so you can come and live with us. Now, time for the zoo."

He seemed very pleased with himself, however, Ruth just wanted to run. She wasn't going to call this woman Mam, she wasn't going to live with her either. And to top it all off, she hated the zoo. She didn't like the animals in cages, they made her sad. Father got out of the car, and so did Cheryl. Ruth reluctantly followed suit. She felt sure that this was going to be a dreadful day, but Mam had been so encouraging, that it gave her strength. When she got home, she could tell Mam all about Cheryl and refuse to ever go off with Father again. If she got home. She clung to the thought that Father had said *getting* a house, which meant they didn't have one yet. She should be safe for the day.

Cheryl leant against the back of the car and lit a cigarette. Father came around to join her, and took one too. They stood closely together, Cheryl rubbing her fish-netted leg against Father's jeaned one. Cheryl looked very happy. Ruth took the time to assess her. She wore far too much make-up. Her skirt was too short and her top too tight. All in all, she looked a bit scary really. The kind of woman that would make a dreadful Mam. The kind of woman that would suit Father down to the ground. *I had the assessment half right, she was the kind of woman that was dreadful, but not the kind*

161

for Father. She was far too mouthy, far too confident. He needed a woman he could belittle and control, not this woman. Around her middle, she had a wide black elastic belt that was clasped at the front with a butterfly made of metal and very colourful. Ruth only ever wore belts if they were to hold her jeans up. She couldn't see what this belt was holding up at all.

"I like your belt," she said, interrupting their moment. "It's very pretty."

Father looked pleased. Clearly, she had said the right thing. Cheryl looked amused, but Ruth couldn't understand why. Cheryl unclasped the belt and bent down to Ruth. She smelt of cloying perfume, something sickly and throat-catching along with stale cigarette smoke. She put the belt around Ruth's middle and clasped it at the front. It didn't sit right because it was far too big, but Cheryl seemed happy. She was laughing.

"Well then you can have it Ruth," she said.

The day at the zoo didn't go so well. Ruth became sadder and sadder the more animals they looked at, eventually, she was on the verge of tears. Cheryl kept trying to get Father's attention by being more and more outrageous. At one point, he threatened to hit her after she swore, but she laughed at him and said he wouldn't dare. Ruth felt like saying, yes, yes he would, but she kept quiet in case he hit her too. When they returned to the car to head back, Ruth sat in the back because she was tired. Cheryl sat next to her and put make-up on her. Ruth just wanted to nap, but she could feel the tension building and so succumbed to the blues and greens quietly. *Eurghhh, I have turned into that. I am the kind of woman that never leaves home without a trowel of paint upon my face. Another thing to change. Once I'm free.*

When they got home, Ruth ran from the car. She didn't even stop to say goodbye. She was frantically ringing the ship's bell before Father had even shut off the ignition. He came after her, and had reached her just as Mam opened the door. Ruth pushed past Mam, ignoring his hands that were scrabbling at the back of her blouse,

162

and stood behind Mam, her arms circling her, holding on for dear life.

"We had a great day, I don't know what's wrong with her," he said.

He walked back down the path and returned to the car. Cheryl was back in the front passenger seat. His face was thunderous. Ruth knew she had upset him, but she didn't care. She never wanted to see him or that woman ever again. Mam stroked her hair as she watched him drive off.

"Let's get this stuff off your face," she said. "That's a pretty belt, did your Dad give it to you?"

Ruth took off the belt in reply and stormed to the kitchen where she shoved it into the bin under the sink. She hated the belt, just like she hated the woman and she hated Father. Mam carried her up to the bathroom, even though she was far too old for that, and helped her scrub her face of all the disgusting colours. Ruth thought Mam looked prettier than Cheryl, and Mam never wore make-up at all.

A few days later, Father called.

"I'm not with Cheryl anymore," he said. *Cilla Black sang Surprise Surprise in my head every time I heard him say the words 'I'm not with...' This was the first, but there were many more. I actually lost count of the amount of marriages, engagements and divorces he had in the end.*

Ruth didn't know what was the best thing to say to that, so she just said "oh."

"It didn't work out, I hope you're not upset, I know you liked her. I know you were looking forward to a new home with us."

Ruth didn't think. She just replaced the handset in the cradle. So that Mam wouldn't find out what she'd done, she also unplugged the cord from the wall. She didn't want Father calling back in a rage. When Mam found out, she'd tell her it was an accident.

25. Ruth

Have you ever felt so lonely that you wanted to step out in front of a car just so that you'd feel the touch of kind human hands. The thought of paramedics, caressing you carefully as they check for injuries, becomes a wish, a hope. I wanted to reach out and hug someone, have someone hug me. Someone hold me without there being something more than sweetness behind the touch. I was scared, I was lonely, I was stupid. I was all of these things and more. I had no other choice, I did, but I had no other choice that I could face. I watched cars driving past the house, and I wished. I hoped.

Bethany woke Ruth up in the morning with a breakfast tray. It had flowers on it and strawberries and cream. She remembered Max giving her the same breakfast after they'd had a fight. It seemed like an age ago, but it couldn't be, it could only have been a couple of months, maybe five. Ruth realised that she'd lost track of time. She didn't even know the date, all she knew was that it was the dreaded day. The wedding day. It felt capitalised in when she thought about it, as though it was permanently on neon duty. THE WEDDING DAY!

"It's going to be lovely Ruth," Bethany said. "Your dress is amazing, and Max is really excited. He's already rung today to check on you."

Ruth smiled wryly at this, she could feel her mind crumbling like a tea-soaked biscuit. Yes, he would be concerned, she thought as she rubbed gently at my black, green and yellow stomach that contained her battered baby. She decided that Bethany had taken her smirk as a smile. Or perhaps, she just chose to ignore the implications. It was hard for Ruth to read people these days, she found that she could no longer look at them, no longer look into their eyes. It was just too much contact with the outside world. She just wanted a crevice, a fissure, to open up for her to crawl into and disappear, alone at last.

164

"You're so lucky Ruth, so lucky. He really loves you, and you love him. He treats you like a Princess." *Snap.*

It was the worst word she could use. It made Ruth take in a breath as though she had been winded, she was gasping and heaving. It was like a physical blow. It was almost worse, because a physical blow could be forgotten eventually, after the evidence faded, but this, this word, would be with her forever. It never faded. Agonising misery ripped through her. Her baby shifted position, reminding her as to why she should stick with the original plan. She was to marry him and hope for the best. She kept saying to herself, 'he'll be fine after the wedding, he's just been stressed out in the lead up to the big day.' *I know I'm wrong, somewhere inside of me, I know I'm wrong.*

Ruth stared at the breakfast until Bethany came back and took it away. It was like being little again. She just could not eat. She felt too confused, frightened, lost. There were too many emotions and thoughts whirling around inside of her, no room for food, for anything else at all. Mam sat on the end of her bed.

"Not much time left my darling, you have to act," she said.

"I don't know how," Ruth replied.

She was right though. Ruth needed to run. It would not be running away, it was not the same. When you ran away from something, or someone, it was because you couldn't, or didn't want to, face them. This would just be running. Running for safety, running to escape. Running to a better place for Ruth and her baby. Not running away, running to. But how would she do it? She had no idea. She just didn't know how she would get past these people, how to get out of the door, how to break free. She was scared of what was outside the door, it had been so long since she had last seen that world, since she had last entered it. *I want to break free.*

Leanna entered the room and Mam disappeared again. The smell of her Tweed perfume lingered on the air she left behind. Ruth knew that just seconds ago, her Mam had really and truly sat with her. It was time to get moving though. Time to prepare for the

165

inevitable. *I wish I'd been able to break through that misted glass. It was in front of my eyes, stopping me from seeing the truth, from seeing reality. I could've just got up that morning and said, 'I'm not doing this.' I could've packed a bag and walked, but the misted glass blinded me and I couldn't see the alternatives.* Leanna and Bethany get her out of bed and into the bath. Ruth could hear Bethany mutter to Leanna outside the door.

"I don't think she's well, maybe we should call Max," she said. *Why?*

"Are you mad?" Leanna asked. "Did you not see the bruises?"

"I only caught a glimpse, she covered them," Bethany said.

"It's probably just pre-wedding jitters," replied Leanna. *Oh why?* "Max is a great man, she probably deserved whatever she got, it doesn't look that bad."

"I doubt that, no one deserves that, Leanna."

Ruth could hear the frown in Bethany's voice. She was confused by Leanna's reaction, by Ruth too. *If only she had really thought about things. If only I had.* Ruth wondered what she was thinking, if she would be like the woman in the dress shop and find her a card with a number to call. As Ruth laid with the bubbles dissipating around her distended stomach and breasts, she wished as hard as she could that she could go back in time and call that number. That she could go back in time and get the hell out. Tears mingled with the steam as they poured down her face, ruining the valiant effort of the mud mask cleansing her skin. Ruth couldn't be cleansed, it was too late. *It wasn't too late, but sometimes, just sometimes, all the world jumbles together and piles on top of you, and you can no longer think. You can no longer see the wood for the trees. I think that they call that depression, no, Depression. It should be capitalised. Like Wedding Day, it is something that requires revere. Like Wedding Day, it is something I hope I have escaped.*

"Well, whatever, it's none of our business. We just need to get her to the church on time."

Ruth managed to get herself ready; she locked the door to the bedroom, shutting Leanna and Bethany out. She found Mam's old bottle of Tweed that she'd had for years and sprayed herself liberally, relishing the memories the scent brought. Although, it was quite vinegary after all that time, as though it shouldn't be worn. Ruth could still smell Tweed, but she wondered if anyone else would, or if she would just smell like chips to them. She looked at her face in the mirror and applied her make-up as carefully as ever. *Oh-so-Cheryl, but without her inner strength.* She got into her dress and fixed her tiara and veil. One of the girls would have to lace her up properly, but that was ok, not too much human contact. She looked at herself *I look at myself, I look at myself but did I see?* in the full-length mirror on the back of the wardrobe door, but she didn't see her reflection. She saw someone pretending to be Ruth; an impostor with red hair and a huge belly. *I didn't see me, but then I didn't see everything either, not the pain, not the desperation.* The wedding dress covered a multitude of sins. Floor length white satin laid over blackened legs and a purple stomach. The girl in the mirror spoke to the girl in the dress.

"You can't do this. I can't do this. If we run, he'll hunt us down. If we hide, he'll find us. If we go through with this, we are signing up for a painful and drawn out suicide pact. We have but one option."

She stared at her face and smiled. One option. One alone. She would *not* marry her father. She could not marry her father. She could not have escaped from one only to repeat it with another. *Snap.*

"I am Ruth Chantry and I am strong. I can do this. I must do this," I tell the scared, pasty white girl in the mirror.

Decision made, she turned to leave the room, to face the music. Bethany knocked the door. *Snap.* Ruth shuddered, unable to walk towards the door for a few seconds. She had made her

167

decision, she would make her escape, but just getting to that door and opening it suddenly felt like an insurmountable task. Eventually, just as Ruth began to hear Bethany calling to the others, clearly still worried, she shuffled one step at a time to the door.

"The car is here Ruth, time to go. Come on hun," she called through the wood.

Ruth checked herself in the mirror once more, surprised that she looked so normal on the outside. Well, normal for a woman on her wedding day. She walked out of the room to the sound of satisfied, if not orgasmic, oohs and aahs of Bethany. She was spun around and laced up as efficiently as if she was still in the wedding dress boutique. Bethany then handed her the bouquet, it was all pink roses, and baby's breath. It made her think of innocence. Sweet remembered innocence that was never ever hers to remember. *I was thinking of my baby, of my baby's innocence. I can't remember an innocence of my own. My earliest memory in this life is of watching my father beat my mother unconscious. I never experienced innocence. I knew things that I should never have known from the first moment I could see.* Bethany hugged Ruth delicately with fluttering hands. Ruth wanted to cling to her, as though she was a drowning woman and only Bethany could save her, but she couldn't do that, so she kept her hands at her sides, immoveable, untouching.

Leanna just glared at her. Even in her self-reflexive state, she realised that Leanna truly looked dreadful. Ruth also realised that Leanna has worn her own shoes with the heels rather than the ballet pumps Ruth had chosen to go with the dress. She didn't really care though, not any more. But she did. As Ruth got in line with her, she stumbled dramatically, using the seconds to stomp on Leanna's toes. She knew, that was the worst thing and yet she thought so little of Ruth. Ruth thought that it was just her making him unhappy, but she learnt in the end. It was nothing to do with her. She could have been any woman in his arms. She could have been Leanna. He was just a bully and a coward. She couldn't tell

168

Leanna, she was the kind of person that had to think these things through and find the answer herself.

Ruth walked past the photographer as he recorded her final moments in film. She walked down the path towards the limousine. *I remember smiling for the camera. I'd love to see that smile. I think it would look horrific. All teeth and no eyes. All pain and no pleasure. But there would be no fear in my eyes or the set of my teeth. I was no longer afraid, but I should have been. I should have been afraid of myself because I had cracked. I wasn't thinking along sane lines.*

She was shocked to see some of the neighbours. They never looked out of their windows, never knocked on the door, when Ruth was screaming as Max beat the shit out of her, but here they are now. Perhaps it was the draw of the limousine, the draw of the wedding party. They were waving and clapping as she walked to the kerb. She didn't know these people, but she hated them all the same. Stood in their living room windows, in their front gardens, to watch the spectacle of Ruth making the stupidest decision of her life. No, not the decision she had just made, but the one that resulted in her being stood there, in that dress. Why, if they were so interested in the goings on of her life, had they never helped her before? She hated those people.

Mam was on the other side of the road, she beckoned Ruth. She flung her bouquet behind her and ran to her Mam. She understood, she could see Ruth's shame and her misery. Mam knew everything. *She doesn't. If she did, her life would've been very, very different. She would never have encouraged me to do what I did either. Never in a million years. I had finally been broken, and so I imagined her there, I imagined her support for something she would never condone.*

"Fuck you all!" Ruth screamed. "Fuck each and every one of you!"

She saw the taxi and she stopped to stare. She watched the driver's face as he shouted, but she didn't hear his words. He

169

covered his face with his arms. *I recognised him too, in those seconds, I remembered him laughing with me because I was going shopping on my anniversary. He was such a nice, cheerful, friendly bloke. It makes me sad that I made such an impact upon his life.*
Ruth's hearing broke free and the squeal of brakes clashed through the silence. She watched gratefully as the car careered towards her, gouging the side of the limousine. She couldn't move, she didn't want to move. Somebody screamed, but it wasn't Ruth, she was, at last, calm. She finally felt peaceful. She had made the right choice this time. She had done the right thing. She didn't feel the car as it hit her, but she heard the snap in my leg. It was over now. Thank God, it was over now. She was free.

She heard the sirens as the ambulance arrives. She heard Leanna telling Bethany that she was going to tell Max, that she was going to have to go to the church because he had turned his mobile off. She heard Bethany sobbing. She heard everything. *I hear everything.* She heard people asking her to open her eyes, they asked her kindly. It was too late, she couldn't open them. She was not ready. She wanted to sleep. She felt the jolt as they loaded her uncommunicative body into the ambulance. Bethany came too. Ruth felt so relieved. So free. She could hear them, but it wouldn't be for much longer. She could feel things, but they were fading. She was drifting. *I am drifting.* She was in and out, moving peacefully away from it all. They stuck needles in her. They opened her eyes and shone lights into her pupils, she felt the warmth, but she was too far along the path to see the light.

But it all went wrong. She was (*I am*) not dead, She was (*I am*) not free. She was (*I am*) still here. She was (*I am*) locked inside myself. She was (*I am*) trapped.

I thought I would die. I am sorry. My poor child, my baby. I was selfish. I did not consider you. I just wanted out. I can't make an excuse, all I can say is I'm sorry. I've ended your life before it started. There were other escapes. Numerous escapes, and instead of the righteous choice, I took the easiest one and you will suffer my mistake too.

But I hear the voices. The baby is still alive. They check the heartbeat. I am still alive and so are you. My body is broken, but it will heal. There is hope. We can go on together. We can be free. *We will be free.*

And this was when the remembering began. My own head, knowing that I had no escape, decided to teach me the lesson that, despite the evidence, I had never learnt. I have watched it all. Nearly all, like a movie, but I can't walk out when it gets too scary. I can't press stop and come back to it later. It is a constant barrage of reliving. I will learn, I have learnt. I know everything. But there is one scene still to go. The one scene that I should've learnt from when it happened. The one scene I have blocked from myself since the very day it happened.

26. Little Ruth

I was almost thirteen by the time I saw him again. The divorce had been finalised, Mam was on the verge of a nervous breakdown from the battle of it all. I didn't know him anymore, and he definitely didn't know me. I was in a different school. I had different interests. I was almost happy.

Mam was cleaning the kitchen, scrubbing out all the cupboards. It reminded Ruth of how she used to be before Father came home. However, this time, she was cleaning because it was spring, the cusp of spring moving into summer. It was warm and sunny, the cold and ice of Winter a distant nightmare. Ruth was sat in the front garden, under the apple tree, with her new book. She listened to Bob whistling as he mowed his lawn next door. It was a wonderful morning at the start of the school holidays. There would be Easter Eggs on Sunday too. In Ruth's opinion, it was turning out to be one of the best days ever.

Mam had taken her to do the shopping first thing in the morning. She had let Ruth spend her pocket money on anything she fancied from the charity shop next to the supermarket. She had chosen a new book. She was allowed any books now because Mam had caught her in the cupboard under the stairs reading a Catherine Cookson book by torch light. She had almost finished it when she was found.

"Where did you get that?" Mam had asked.

"From your cupboard. I was bored, I've read all my books."

"It's not suitable for a little girl."

"I really like it."

"Well, you had better finish reading it, or I'll never get any peace until you do."

"Can I ask you a question?"

"Is it about the book?"

"Kind of."

"Go on then," Mam sighed.

172

"What's rape?"

After Mam had explained, Ruth felt really old and very sad.

"Men are horrible, aren't they?"

"Not all men."

Ruth decided that she wasn't sure Mam was right. Uncle Bob was ok, but Ruth's knowledge of men was limited to him and to her own Father. Unfortunately, the knowledge of that man outweighed anything else, and so her opinion of all men was rather tainted these days. After that though, she was allowed to read whatever she liked.

"There's not a lot worse in this world than rape, so I guess if you've read about that, there's not a lot worse in any book that you could read," said Mam. She had closed the cupboard door behind her with another sigh.

Ruth's new book was called *The Dead Zone*. It had cost her fifty pence. She had chosen that one because she liked the front cover. It was a picture of a hand, palm out as if to say "STOP!" In the centre of the hand, there was a cross. The picture was shaded in different blues so that it looked like light was shining out of it. The lady in the shop had called it a "horror book" and had refused to sell it to her until Mam came in and said it was ok.

Mam had been unsure, but Ruth had won her round. She told Mam that she had already read *IT* by the same author and she hadn't been *that* scared. She promised to only read the new book if the sun was shining. Mam gave in then. The lady in the shop had pursed her lips in a very disapproving way and put the book into a bag. She passed it to Mam as if she didn't want to be seen selling books like that to children.

Ruth started to read and was hooked from the first sentence. *That became my all time favourite book – ironic really.* She became so lost in the story that the world around her disappeared. Even the steady sounds of the birth of summer faded into a background drone that she could ignore.

"What are you reading, Princess?"

173

She pulled herself out of the book, blinking as reality returned her senses and she found herself still sat in a sunny garden, and not skating on an icy pond. Father was stood on the other side of the garden wall. She hoped that Bob was still in his front garden too, but the sound of his lawn mower had stopped.

"A book," she replied.

He didn't look like Father. He was clean-shaven, and he'd lost a lot of weight from his face and his tummy. His eyes were the same though; a bright sparkling blue that always seemed on the edge of rage.

"I can see that," he laughed. "What book is it?"

"*The Dead Zone.*"

"I don't know that one, who's it by?"

"Stephen King."

"Is Mam at home?"

"She's in the kitchen."

He jumped over the wall and marched through the garden. The front door was open, he went straight into the house. Ruth stood up and looked over the hedge. Bob was still in his garden, he stood leaning on his spade.

"It's alright Ruth, I'll just let Jean know I'm coming over," he said as an ear-splitting scream followed by a thud came from the kitchen of Ruth's home.

Ruth didn't know whether to scream, cry or run in the house. She opted for all three and barged into the kitchen. Mam was cowering on the floor in a corner between two cupboards. Father was standing over her with his fist raised in the air. He turned as she charged through the kitchen door, screaming as loud as she could.

"It's ok, me and Mam are just having a chat."

She ran past him to Mam and stood between them.

"Don't hit my Mam," she said.

"I didn't, she just fell over, that was all."

Ruth didn't believe him. She stood her ground. She was too small to stop him before, but she had grown. She could try. And she

174

had had enough of memories that haunted her at three in the morning of seeing her Mam unconscious, suffering. She had plenty of those, no need to add more.

He grabbed her by her arms and threw her to the side. She hit the table and fell over. She watched as he reached down to Mam and pulled her to her feet by the front of her dress. The dress tore a little, but not enough to let her escape. He raised his fist and punched her again. Her had swung back and hit the cabinet. Ruth knew he'd knocked her unconscious. Again. She just wanted to kill him, but still, in that swish of bile in her stomach, she knew she loved him. Why couldn't he just be normal? Why couldn't he just treat Mam properly?

"Lay Val down gently Rick, you've done all the damage you can."

Ruth turned away from Father and saw Bob standing in the doorway. He still had his shovel in his hand. *I had always seen Bob as a gentle person, but I remember seeing him with that shovel and feeling very scared. He looked so menacing.* He didn't look at Ruth, nor Mam. He kept his eyes focused on Father.

"Come on now Rick, enough is enough."

"She's my wife."

"No, she's not, and even if she were, it's not right to hit a woman."

Father dropped Mam onto the floor. Ruth watched as her head lolled to one side and blood dribbled down from the corner of her mouth. She wanted to be back in the garden with her book. A horror story was far less scary than what was taking place in her kitchen. She wanted to go to Mam, but she was frightened that Father might throw her again, and her chest was still very painful from the last time.

She gazed at her Mam, hoping and praying that she was all right. From the corner of her eye, she saw Father look at her. He seemed to be sizing her up, as if she was next. She turned to face him full on and didn't drop her eyes. She didn't want him to see she was scared.

175

"She just makes me so angry Ruth, it's her own fault."

Ruth didn't reply. *If only I'd been able to say something, to tell him what he'd done and why. He'd never have understood though, he was too far gone down the path of alcoholism for sense to break through. I think his brain was turning to mush even then.* He turned and walked to the door, went past Bob and out to the garden. Ruth ran to go after him. She wanted to tear him apart, Bob caught her before she could get by.

"He just isn't worth it Ruth, come on, let's help Mam."

Ruth could hear sirens close by. She prayed that they were police sirens coming for Father. She went with Bob to where Mam lay.

"She's still breathing, Ruth."

A car engine started outside, she turned and caught a glimpse of Father driving away. Seconds later a police car and an ambulance arrived and Jean came to take Ruth to her home.

Mam left hospital a week later. She told Ruth that there had been no permanent damage done. She took Ruth to the police station with her when she made a statement and took out an injunction against Father. Mam explained what an injunction was. Ruth thought that she had never heard of such an amazing and wonderful law in all her life. The police said that they hadn't found Father yet, but that they would keep looking. They were going to arrest him when they did find him. Mam thanked them politely and took Ruth home on the bus. She'd finally managed to get a car a few months before, but she wasn't allowed to drive it for a while because of the hits to her head.

When they arrived home, a parcel had been delivered for Ruth. She didn't recognise the writing, but Mam did.

"Oh God no, why won't he just leave us alone," she said.

Ruth opened the package, and inside was a book wrapped in what seemed like tracing paper. She found a note stuck to the paper.

"Tell Mam I'm sorry. I bought you something more suitable for a little girl to read."

Ruth felt that she had never felt less like a little girl, but proceeded to take the book out of the paper. It was the complete works of Lewis Carroll. She looked at the picture on the front of rabbits wearing clocks and smiling cats. It didn't look like something she might like, but it was a book, so in her eyes, it needed to be read. She made Mam a cup of tea and sat down to read.

She had read the first chapter when the phone rang. Mam went to answer it. She didn't speak into the phone, she just started crying. Ruth waited, watching her. Mam just held the phone against her ear and sobbed into the mouthpiece. Ruth went to her and reached up to pull the phone cord. As soon as she tugged it, the handset fell from Mam's hand. Ruth caught it and said hello.

"Hello Princess, did you get your book?"

"Yes thank you."

"It's much better than that crap you were reading."

"I think it's horrible. Did you keep the receipt?"

Father was silent for a moment.

"Is Mam still crying?"

Ruth put the phone down. Mam slid down the cabinet and sobbed in a crumpled heap on the floor. To Ruth, it seemed that Mam had finally drifted over the edge to a new place. *I had never felt so alone and so young as I did at that moment. But I grew up, I had to. And now I truly understand because I've been to that place too.* She went upstairs and started running off a bath for Mam. She added lots of bubbles. She wasn't sure that she could change Mam's sheets, but she decided she could try. The bed was huge compared to her own, so it would be a bit difficult. It took her half an hour, but finally it was done. The quilt was in a clean cover, although it was a bit lumpy; the pillows were in pillow cases, just not the usual matching ones and the sheet was on the mattress, at a bit of an angle. She had turned off the bath taps half way through so as not to make a flood. She went and checked the water was still warm and added a few more bubbles for good measure. Ruth went downstairs and found Mam exactly as she'd left her.

177

"Come on Mam, up you get now."

She pushed and pulled until Mam was finally on her feet. Mam wobbled a bit, so Ruth got behind her and pushed her in the direction of the stairs. She ignored Mam's grumblings and kept on pushing until finally she had her in the bathroom.

"Clothes off Mam," she said.

Mam had started to cry again as soon as she saw the bath. Ruth had to fight to get her out of her clothes and into the water, but she managed it. She helped Mam wash her back and hair. Mam even smiled. *That day was so hard. Maybe if I could have said all this to Max he would have understood me better, he would've stopped. Maybe it's not too late, not yet. No, it never works like that. He'd think that Father was in the right. He would never understand, it's time for me to let go.*

Mam got herself out of the bath. She went into the bedroom and put on the clean nightie Ruth had laid out for her, she got into bed and fell asleep almost immediately. Ruth went to her room and tidied it up. She hid her dirty clothes so that no one would know that Mam hadn't done any washing recently.

The next day, Mam said they were going to the beach. Just as they were packing the towels and swimsuits into carrier bags, the doorbell rang. Mam went to the door. She didn't look so cheerful when she returned to the kitchen with a lady Ruth had never seen before.

"This is Mrs Lane, she's from Social Services. Go and play in the living room while I have a chat to Mrs Lane and then we can go to the beach."

Ruth left the kitchen but stayed next to the door.

"Your husband has made a complaint Mrs Ellis. He thinks you are incapable of caring for Ruth."

"I think you'll find he is the one that's incapable. Did he tell you he came to visit Ruth and put me in the hospital for a week? Did he tell you she witnessed the whole thing? Did he tell you that

178

the police are looking for him? I took an injunction out against him to protect Ruth, to keep her safe from him, did he mention that?"

"Well, I can check into all of that when I return to the office, but I'm sure you appreciate that these matters have to be looked into when a complaint such as this is made, may I have a look at your daughter's bedroom?"

Ruth ran into the living room just as the two women came through the kitchen door. She listened as they went upstairs. She could tell Mam was showing the lady all the bedrooms and the bathroom. They came back downstairs.

"Right, if I may just have a word with Ruth before I leave."

Ruth dived onto the settee and tried to make it look like she was in a comfortable position.

"Hello Ruth, I'm Mrs Lane."

Mam hovered behind the lady but didn't come and sit with Ruth. *He was an evil bastard. He couldn't make me want to be with him, so he tried to get someone else to do it. I hate him.*

"Hello," Ruth replied.

"I just want to ask you a few questions, will that be ok?"

"I suppose so, but I want my Mam sat with me."

Mrs Lane smiled and beckoned Mam with her finger. Mam came and sat on the settee next to Ruth and put her arm around her.

"Right, now you're comfortable, are you happy living with your Mummy?" asked Mrs Lane.

"Yes."

"Would you like to go and stay with your Daddy for a little while?"

"No."

"Would you like it if Daddy came home to stay with you and Mummy for a little while?"

"No, definitely not."

"Are you ever frightened of Mummy?"

"No, but I'm scared of Father."

"Right, well, do you know how to use a telephone?"

179

"Of course." *How old did she think I was? She spoke to me the whole time as though I was a fool, or perhaps a toddler. I think she was in the wrong job entirely.*

"Ok, here is my number," she produced a card from her bag and gave it to Ruth. "Call that number if you need some help, if you get scared or anything at all."

"If Father comes back, the policeman said to just ring 999 and that's what I'll do."

"Well, keep that just in case it's not Father that worries you."

Ruth took the card. She wanted the lady to leave. She could feel Mam's hand trembling against her waist. Mrs Lane stood up, Mam stood up with her. Ruth watched as they left the room and listened as they said their goodbyes. She felt she had never hated anyone in the world as much as she hated Father. Mam returned to the living room.

"I think we should go to the shop today and get some food instead of going to the beach, ok?"

"Yes Mam."

I could never forgive my father. I knew even then what he was doing and I loathed him for it. I tore the card into little pieces and kept it in my purse. Every time we went somewhere, I dropped another little bit. I wanted that card to be so scattered that no one would ever piece it together again.

27. The Wedding

This is how imagine what happened. But I doubt it. Leanne would never have been that upset. And the telling would never have been so contrived, but if anything did happen, then this is what I would've wanted. The shock, the awe, the drama. The proof that people did actually care for me.

People fidgeted on the polished pews crammed between opulent flower arrangements. Snow fell steadily outside, and within the Church it was just as cold, if not more so.

The groom leaned towards his best man and muttered, "Twenty minutes now, she'd be late for her own funeral."

The best man smirked in acknowledgment. Family and friends checked their watches while the organist kept time in interlude music, bored to death, waiting to play the wedding march.

The entrance doors burst open and the Maid of Honour came running down the aisle. The organist stopped playing, the chaplain smiled benevolently and the congregation stood in united relief. She reached the altar, and grabbed the groom as he and the best man stood up expectantly.

"An accident, Ruth's in the hospital."

The threesome pelted back up the aisle and out of the Church. Whispers of confusion followed them in a rushing roar.

28. Max

I never made that phone call either. That was all a lie. I was talking to the dialling tone. I was so frightened in case you didn't believe me and tried last number redial. It would have brought up something else, but not Leanna. I never called her. And then you were so nice about it, and you said you wanted Leanna as part of the wedding. I would have said no if I'd known what you were up to, but I didn't. And I got stuck in between you, fighting with each other, over me, over a dress. It was so hard, like living two lives. And it was all your fault, but I was the one in the wrong.

Leanna did really plant that necklace though. I don't know when she did it, but it was done on purpose. She wanted us to break up because I had told her that one day we would, and then Leanna and I could be together. I was stringing her along, I know it, but I just couldn't live without her. I needed her there with me. It was a nightmare trying to live two lives at once. She hated being involved in the wedding. It drove her mad. It was all she could talk about each time we met. I often wondered if you were doing that to be malicious, but then I think it was my own paranoia. Developed from my own behaviour.

It's so hard now. Fletch talks about their renewed love all the time. How they're really making a go of it this time. How he's changed. No more clubbing for him. I think it's all a load of crap to be honest. I don't think those two will ever change. He'll keep on cheating on her and she'll keep on pretending he isn't. She just wants to be with someone. I'd prefer to be alone than to be with someone that cheats all the time. I know it isn't much, but Leanna is the only time I ever cheated on you. It's the only time she ever cheated on Fletch too. Or at least that's what she said. I really regret it. I really do. I wish I could make it up to you. I wish I could turn back the clock and start again.

I am so proud of you. The improvements this week have been brilliant. Here, let me give you a kiss. No response, but, squeeze my hand, go on, do it. Ok, not as good as last night, but still, you're doing well. Anyway, we are almost at the end of *Philosopher's Stone*. I'm going to read this to our child as he or she grows up, we can all read it together, as a family. You and me with baby (or toddler, or child, or teen) sitting in between us on the sofa, book in hand.

Harry swallowed and looked around him. He realised he must be in the hospital wing.
...
'How long have I been in here?'
'Three days. Mr Ronald Weasley and Miss Granger will be most relieved you have come round, they have been extremely worried.'

That'll be you, that will. You'll come round and we'll all be most relieved. Have you been with Harry, my love? God I'm talking doo-lally now. I think it's time you woke up before I get carted off with the men in white coats. I wish we could talk about the stories. Like we used to. Do you remember, when we first met, all that time ago. I saw you sitting outside a Costa Coffee, brazenly reading *Lolita* and not caring if people looked when you laughed, or if you cried. You were so engrossed. And I saw you giggle. So I asked you what was so funny. You said that it was the hardest book to read because it caught your sense of humour and made you laugh and then you remembered what the story was about and it made you feel guilty for laughing. You recommended I read it. Then you gave me your copy with your phone number on a slip of paper inside. We would talk about books all the time back then.
I can't believe how hard you're trying. I saw your eyes flicker today and I was so excited, I ran into the corridor and told the first person I met. "Her eyes flickered!" I shouted into his face. Unfortunately, he was a cleaner and didn't have a clue what I was on about, nor did he care. I was so excited, I had to tell someone. They still don't reckon
183

you'll be well enough to have the baby normally though. The doctor said that even if you were, you'd probably still need a caesarean because your hips are so small and our baby is a really good size.

It's been a long old slog. I nearly gave up sometimes. But I love you so much, that I never thought really that I'd give in. You are all that I have. You and our baby. I mean, I know I have friends and family. I know that you have no family left, but still. I know what I mean. Are you excited? We'll know if it's a boy or a girl soon. What names did we decide on? Was it Jezebel for a girl, like the woman in the bible, the one that was a faithful and loyal wife, I remember discussing that. All the different meanings for one name. Now, was it Ciaran for a boy? No, you didn't like either of those did you? I remember now. You didn't like the names I'd chosen. Your names were Jeremy Luke for a boy, Victoria Louise for a girl. You'll wake up to see our baby though won't you? I can't believe that you wouldn't want to be awake when our baby is born.

Keep trying my love, you're nearly here.

29. Little Ruth

Sometimes, things happen. You can't change them. You can't do anything about them. They've already happened and there's no going back. However, that doesn't stop you having them in your head for all time. It doesn't stop you from thinking every single day, if only... There are lots of things about that day, the worst day of my entire life, where I think, if only. If only I'd rung Mam, if only I hadn't stayed in college so long. If only, if only. It'll be with me until the day I die.

Ruth had had a great day at college. She'd finally finished her university application forms. It had taken her months, mainly because she couldn't decide where to go or what to do. Advice had come from all corners. Everyone she'd ever met seemed to want to give her their thoughts on what would be best. In the end, she'd opted for Law with French. She was good at French, and she felt that as a lawyer, perhaps she could help people. People like Mam who were going through messy divorces and needed someone to fight their corner. Someone on their side.

She had finally decided to apply to six universities that were within commuting distance. Although she wanted to live in halls and to have the full university experience, she wanted to be able to come home at the drop of a hat. She hadn't forgotten about Father. They hadn't heard from him for years, but memories are stronger than people give them credit. They can control a girl's life choices permanently.

She couldn't wait to get home and tell Mam, she knew she would be so pleased. It would mean the world to her that Ruth was making a better future for herself. That Ruth was going to be self-sufficient and educated. *I should've continued after everything happened, but that hopeful, promising part of me died that day. Perhaps I can find it again. It's still not too late, not even now.*

She had got the ten past five bus, but instead of ringing Mam for a lift from the bus stop, which was what Mam liked her to do

185

when it was dark, she had decided to take the twenty minute walk. By the time she turned the corner at the end of the street, it was quarter past six and truly dark. She loved this time of year. January was the time when new beginnings should be made. When the past is behind yet another New Year's party. Behind another midnight count down.

Ten feet into the road and she stopped. There was a car parked in front of her house. It shone in the acidity of the street lamp. Ruth recognised it. He hadn't changed his car. It was the same one he had been driving the day she was reading *The Dead Zone*. Her breath caught in her throat, her heart hammered like there was a drill pumping it. *I could've run away then, but that would have been running away, not running, but definitely running away.*

She walked slowly toward the house. Whatever was going on inside wouldn't stop if she ran. As she came in line with the living room window, she saw the back of his head in the chair, the television was on, and the silhouette was created through its colourful hues of changing images. He seemed to be sat comfortably. Ruth stood silently in the shadows watching him, waiting. She didn't want to think about what she was waiting for, but it was there in her mind, drifting, bouncing off the walls, but never becoming a fully formed thought. She was waiting to see Mam's silhouette cross the window.

After half an hour, nothing had happened. He hadn't moved, Mam hadn't walked past any of the windows in the front. Ruth was still stood on the pavement watching and waiting. She was too scared to go in. The lack of Mam's shadow scared her more than anything. Her hands shook, but she wasn't sure if it was with cold or terror. She could stand it no longer.

She walked past the gate and on down the road to the phone box. She would be safe about this. She was sure Mam was alright. *But I wasn't. I knew. The second I had seen the car I knew. I knew it was too late. I knew that if I hadn't stayed on at college and had come home at half two like I should have done, then he wouldn't be*

186

there and Mam would. I could've made things different. Or could I? She dialled nine nine nine.

"Emergency services, how may I help?"

"Police please."

"Putting you through."

"Police?"

"Hi, my name is Ruth Chantry. My Mam is in our house, but I haven't seen her move through the window. My Father is in there also. He is a violent alcoholic. We haven't seen him for years, maybe four or five, I know he's done something to her, please come quickly. Please save her."

As she said the last bit, her voice cracked. Tears began to stream down her face because she knew it was too late. She gave the operator her address and listened to her instructions. Not to approach the house. Not to go inside. To stay away. If he came out, to hide from him. Ruth listened carefully and then walked back to the house and waited outside. He hadn't moved. By the time the police car arrived, her fingers were blue.

It was all so surreal, and in a way, it was an anti-climax. The police car arrived alone, no flashing lights, no sirens. There were two male police officers. One talked to Ruth, asking her to tell him exactly what had happened so far. The other one went to the front door and started ringing the bell and banging the letter box. Ruth watched the living room window as he did this. There was no sign of movement. A small hidden part of her took that moment to wish he was dead. To hope that he had killed himself in the chair in front of the television. But this part of her was very quiet. Almost silent, because the main part of her still loved him. Hated him, but loved him. That had not changed as yet.

The officer that had gone to the door returned to them. He looked serious and concerned. His face made Ruth nauseous.

"No answer, do you have a key love?"

"No, I've never needed one," Ruth said, suddenly wondering why at nearly eighteen years old she still didn't have a key. They had a safe neighbourhood, Mam often left the door on the latch.

"We'll need an enforcer," he said to the other officer before walking off, his radio held to his mouth.

The shadow in the living room still had not moved. Ruth couldn't focus on what the first officer was saying to her. She was sure it was important, but her ears seemed to be blocking everything out. *That still happens to me. I block everything out so that I don't have to experience the truth. So that I don't have to know.* Her sight seemed to be the only one of her senses that was working, and it was working in overdrive, taking in every nuance, every sliver of light, every area of darkness, every movement of every twig in the breeze. She saw him stand.

"He's coming," she said.

The officer turned to face the house, trying to see what she could see. Another police car arrived, and he opened the front door. The officer that had been talking to Ruth jumped over the wall and ran to the door, the other officer was with him so quickly that Ruth hadn't even seen where he had come from. Two more officers followed within seconds, the engine of their car still running, the blue lights now flashing, as they had arrived with more urgency.

Ruth's ears reopened, the scene was bathed in a surreal blue light. Three police officers held Father pinned to the wall of the house, the fourth was stepping over the threshold when he spoke.

"I did it. I killed her." *At those words, the dichotomy inside me was reunited into one whole. One whole of hatred. And I could've died myself. My heart stopped brating, my lungs forgot to work. Everything in my world was still. Everything was dead. And he was stood there, looking directly at me. There was no sympathy, no apology, nothing but fear in his face. He looked at me and I collapsed. I couldn't even return the stare. I could do nothing.*

The officers froze. Ruth crumpled onto the rough, dirty pavement. Neighbours were appearing. At some point, they took

188

him, him that would never have a name for Ruth again, past her and put him into the back of a van that had miraculously appeared. She stayed in her small space on the ground. She stayed with her legs twisted underneath her, her hands at her throat. She could feel the physical numbness pushing through her body, followed closely by emotions that washed over her before shutting down one by one until she was entirely numb. Floodlights appeared from nowhere. Camera flashes followed. Who would want photos? She couldn't think of a worse picture. A picture that no one would ever want to see. Why did they want photos? Things happened around her that she missed. Her Mam's body was taken away. She didn't even get to say goodbye. She didn't see her leave. *Part of me insisted it was all a lie, that it was all a dream. That at any second, I would wake up and Mam would be downstairs at the kitchen table drinking her coffee and staring out the window at the back garden, where she always was in the morning.*

At some indistinguishable point, when all the lights were still going, all the blue and the white that was taking over her being, someone came and helped her to stand. They put her in the back of a police car, and as the neighbours looked on, they drove her away. She did not cry. There were no tears that could accommodate her pain, nothing that could break through her numbness. They drove her to a hotel and checked her in. They put her in a room. A comfy room with Victorian decor that felt homely. They left a female police officer at the door in case she needed anything. They told her to sleep.

By this time, it was half three in the morning, but Ruth could not sleep. She had been awake for nearly twenty four hours, the most difficult and unexpected twenty four hours of her life. She'd give anything to go back to the start of that time period and change everything. *Nothing has ever changed there I can change nothing at all and I never will be able to either.* There was everything inside her that needed to be quietened, but yet every part of her seemed so shut off, there was nothing there to quiet. She lay on the bed in her

189

t-shirt and knickers that she'd been wearing all day and stared at the ceiling, since she had dressed at seven o'clock the previous day. She was still there in the same position, staring at the same spot, when there was a knock at the door in the morning. It had been exactly twenty four hours since she had last slept. Exactly twenty four hours since the worst day of her life had begun. It was over now.

Everything in the world was so surreal. Nothing seemed to be true, to hold reality. It felt like sand, slipping through my fingers, and I couldn't change a thing. I know now, now that I've had time to mature, to grow older, to experience, that even if I had been there, nothing would be different. Perhaps the only difference might be that I had been killed along side Mam. I think he had finally lost it. I learnt at the court case that he thought she had met someone else because he'd seen her in the street talking and laughing with a man he didn't know, and he had snapped. She had done nothing of the sort, and even if she had, it was none of his damned business. He divorced her. He had the affairs. She did nothing but love him.

A woman came in with some clothes and some breakfast. She was motherly, friendly. Ruth had no idea who she was, but didn't object. The woman bustled, and that was just what Ruth needed. She got Ruth into the bathroom and stood outside the door to listen to her shower. To make sure that she did. She gave Ruth clothes to dress in. Not Ruth's clothes, alien clothes. The woman told her in her never-ending story way that she had heard what had happened and as she was a chamber maid at the hotel where the police usually brought victims, she had taken some of her daughter's clothes and brought them to work. The only thing that really made it through the soup was the word victim. Ruth didn't like the sound of that word. She didn't like its connotations.

The woman sat on the end of the bed while Ruth drank a bit of tea and ate a mouthful of toast. She couldn't eat anymore after that, she felt too sick. Everything, even the weak sunshine, made her feel sick. Her whole world had been wrenched out from underneath her feet. There was nothing left except nausea.

190

Eventually, a police officer came to the door and took her to an office behind the hotel's reception. She was greeted by a man in a dark suit and another female officer. He introduced them both, however, the information seemed to get lost before it made it to her brain. He made her talk about everything, and she told him everything in a slow, monotonous voice. At one point, her stopped the interview and took the woman outside. Ruth could hear him panicking about something.

"Sorry Ruth, we just had a moment, something you said there, made us think that perhaps you thought your Mum was still alive. She couldn't have been saved you know, even if we had been on the scene the second it happened. He had stabbed her too many times."

Instead of thinking about what he was saying, she focused upon what she had said. Finally, she realised that she had mentioned that Mam often left the door open, and had then worried aloud about if her Mam would be in trouble for doing that, if it would change things, let him get away with it or something. It had occurred to her that perhaps it was illegal to leave your door open or something. She now realised that Mam would never be in trouble ever again. She still didn't cry.

After the questions had finished, the man left her alone with the woman. They had more tea. Ruth stared at the wall.

"You're safe now," she said.

"So is Mam," Ruth replied.

It was then that she cried. *And have never moved on, never learnt. I owe an apology to you Mam. I should never have let your life, your death, be in vain. I should've learnt from what happened and never made the same mistakes. But I didn't. I didn't even go to university like you so desperately wanted me to, no, I did nothing. I had the house cleaned, I rented it out, have done ever since, and I never went back. I never revisited my past to see what it could teach me. Now I have. Now I will make you proud Mam. I will do everything to make you proud.*

191

30. Max

I sat here all last night willing you to open your eyes. I'm sitting here this morning, pushing for the same thing. Ruth, I need you here with me. I can't go through this alone. I mean what more can I do to help you? I feel like leaping onto the bed and shaking you until you open your damn eyes. I know that'd do more harm than good, but I'm still struggling to restrain myself. I want you. I need you. Why are you being so damned selfish? Think of me for a change, and how I'm suffering. You in your peaceful world of noncommittal unconsciousness. Me watching you. I am the one suffering here. Can't you see that? Won't you give me a break?

I don't get what brought you here anyway. Fletch talked to Leanna and said that you saw the car. That you stood in its path. Was that a suicide attempt? Apparently, you shouted something along the lines of 'Fuck you all!' Interesting. How can I even voice that question? When can I get an answer? There was nothing wrong with you. I would have noticed if you were depressed. I mean you weren't yourself, but that was to be expected. You were heavily pregnant and about to get married. And forever winding me up and suffering the payback. If only you could have been better about the house, you knew I was stressed out. Why couldn't you just talk to me? Or to anyone.

I mean, I know we stopped communicating, as in the self-help book way, after that fight, but I never thought that would stop us from talking about something serious. I regretted every second of that fight. It was all because I was so hung up on Leanna without meaning to be that I got angry. Angry about a stupid bloody dress and a ridiculous lie. I knew she was trying to split us up. I should never have believed a word she said. And then I did the thing that I will never forgive myself for. I hit you for Leanna's behaviour. The pain that caused me. You became so introverted. I know I've just said that there was nothing wrong with you, but there was. I saw it and just ignored it. I was so wrapped up in my own life, that I didn't

192

want to try and delve into yours. It's my fault. I could've talked to you. Tried to make things right.

Should I have called off the wedding? I almost did. When Leanna told me you had been sleeping with Fletch, but both you and Fletch denied it with such honesty that I knew she was just trying to stir. But part of me wanted to believe she was telling the truth. Pre-wedding jitters I guess, but even so, I can't believe that I believed. I knew she was lying. I treated you like shit though, didn't I? I should have known that you loved me too much to ever cheat on me. That I was the worthless one. What angers me most now is that if I hadn't been so selfish then I could have helped you. None of this would have happened, and I wouldn't be sat here talking to you in the hopes that at some point you'll reply. I mean if I'd loved you as much as you loved me. I should have called off the wedding. You stepped out in front of that car because you couldn't take any more of me. I'll never forgive myself for that. Not for as long as I live.

Listen to me. Sitting here all morose. I should be joyful. Our baby's coming, and you're getting better. I know you didn't want to be hit by that cab. I know it wasn't planned or anything. It was an accident. I'm sorry I said all that. Do you reckon there'll ever be a day when I think before I speak? A day when I can stop apologising for being me? I'm sorry. I love you Ruth. Not long now and you'll be ok. Everything will be ok. We can move into our nice new house with our nice new baby and live a nice new life. Maybe we can get married next year, huh? Plan it properly this time. And we won't invite Leanna.

I think that you should join a group of some sort. Get some friends that like the same stuff you do, instead of my friends, who like the same stuff I do. Maybe a book group. They're popular at the moment, I've seen loads of adverts. And you like books, you used to talk about them for hours. I know that was a long time ago. Maybe you could go to college or something. I don't know. But what I do know is that when you're better, we'll make time for you, time for you to do something you love.

193

31. Max

Tomorrow is the day. I'm all over the shop. I'm excited, nervous, scared, happy. And you, so proud of you. I saw you open your eyes today, just a smidgen, just enough for me to see the beauty beneath those eyelids and then you closed them again. But it was enough. It proved to me that you're fighting.

I've thought a lot about what I said yesterday. I called Bethany and asked her to tell me exactly what happened. She said that you really weren't right. You'd gone to bed early without saying goodnight, and that when she woke you up in the morning, you didn't speak to her, but seemed to mumble to the corner of the room. As though there was someone there. She wanted to call me, but Leanna said it was just pre-wedding nerves. She was so sorry she didn't call.

She said that you walked through the house with your head held high, reeking of Tweed perfume. You'd put so much on, it nearly made her gag. Why did you do that? Then you went out to the limousine and suddenly screamed, "Fuck you all! Fuck each and every one of you!" That was when you ran into the road. You saw the taxi, you waited calmly for it to hit you. Why did you do that? Why didn't you step back from the taxi? Bethany said you had time, but you just waited.

Why didn't you tell me you were sad? Why didn't you talk to me? It's my fault isn't it? All my fault. I knew you weren't right, but I just thought it was nerves. And Leanna. I'm sorry that went on. But you wouldn't make love to me and I needed to be loved. I almost destroyed you, I'm so sorry. Leanna, it wasn't her fault, I lied to her as much as I lied to you. I'm sorry, I wish I could turn back time. I almost destroyed you. But when you're better, we can make a fresh start. If you'll forgive me that is.

We'll get help, you and me. Go to counselling together, work through our problems. It'll all be ok in the end. You've made so much progress, I can't believe that you won't want to make more when you wake up. We'll try together. We'll be the perfect family.

32. The Birth

Perfection was what made it all go wrong in the first place. I think you need to know that. I see the light. It flashes over my eyes in red streaks.

Epidural please.

I hear them talking, this is it. I bring my mouth into a smile, or as close as I can to a smile. I'm at the end, I'm so close.

It'll be all right Ruth. Don't you worry.

My baby's coming. At last I feel aware, not distant. I know what's happening.

Scalpel.

I can't feel my legs. The epidural is working I guess. Oh my God what was that? Oh fuck. It feels like someone is washing up the dishes in my stomach. What the hell? Stop! STOP! I want to be awake for my baby, let me be awake.

There's the head, how's she doing? Good girl Ruth.

Oh my God, this is horrible, oh I feel sick.

There's a lot of blood.

I'm floating along in a boat on the sea. Make it stop, oh my God, is that my baby? Is that mine?

It's a girl. The father's going to have a shock though. Where is all that blood coming from? There must be a tear somewhere.

I can hear my baby, she's a girl. I want to call her Rebecca. No, Jennifer. No, Valerie, after Mam. Perfect name for a perfect girl.

She's tachycardic. We're losing her. Hang on Ruth, hang in there sweetheart.

33. Ruth

I come around, but not in the right way. I can feel that I am breathing. I can feel my legs again. My stomach is sore. Very, very sore indeed. I remember the birth in a way, I remember the fear. I remember hearing Valerie cry, but I didn't see her. I didn't see anything at all. I really want to see her, but I am still in that world of darkness where memories torment me into submission, into change. I have nothing left to remember. I've done it all, I've made my choices. I've worked through the issues that lead me to that decision, that day.

I remember them being worried, the voices that is, telling me to hang on. It makes me smile, although apparently only internally, as I do nothing else, I can't feel the corners of my mouth rise, no matter how much I will them to do so. I have to live for my daughter. I have to be there for her. I have to give her a life. A better life than mine. I wonder now if Mam had been in the same position as me when she had me. I wonder if she was bruised and battered. I wonder if she felt as protective at the sound of my first cry. I wish I could ask her. I no longer want to imagine her sitting on the end of my bed though because that doesn't help. It makes everything so much more difficult.

It's time for me to sort myself out, to get some help. Time for me to make my effort. I need to be here, whole, for my daughter. I start with my toes. This will be a continuous process, hard work, but necessary. I have to start somewhere though, and my toes, being the furthest point from my battered and bruised conscious are the beginning.

I visualise them as separate entities, apart from the rest of my body. I imagine each one as an individual item. With each wiggle in my mind, I make a promise. I promise that this is the change. I promise that this situation will not reoccur; I promise that I have learnt. I visualise my toes reattached to my feet. My feet are alone, but I will not be. I have my daughter. I will survive and not only survive, I will live. I roll the balls of my feet.

The feet reattach to my shins. Long, smooth pale shins. I feel the blood coursing through them, and with each pump, I make more promises. I will amend my wasted years. I will protect my daughter from the life I've lead. Valerie will not suffer the pain I have. She will not experience my beaten body being carried away in a black sack. She will never wear blue plastic over her shoes so as not to affect evidence. My shins shiver and reattach to my knees and thighs.

The muscles in my thighs twitch and shift, as if they are finding out what they are supposed to be doing. Trying to rediscover their purpose and existence. As am I. My purpose is to avenge the death of my mother by being strong and wise. By not repeating her mistakes any longer. I will be somebody in my own right. I will exist and be.

My thighs ache as they connect to my hips and abdomen. The pain from my caesarean is luscious. It contains life. Life for me and for my girl. A new life, one where we are *both* safe. We can go anywhere and do anything. We have money, I have some education, I can do more. We are joined together and it is my mission, my task, to ensure that Valerie never has to make these decisions.

My focus shifts to my fingers. Fingers that have been lax for so long, and not used for their purpose. To touch, to love, to caress, to hold, to defend. None of these things have been done with my fingers. Not in the way they are meant to be done anyway. I flex each knuckle. They have removed my engagement ring. I am thankful for that. It was a decision taken from me, but still one that I approve. I shall never wear that ring again. But this is the time to accept that not all men are my father. There are millions of men out there in the world that are loving and kind. I promise that I shall not tar all with the same brush, but that should I meet someone new, I will approach with caution. I will allow myself to love again, but not to live in fear and pain.

198

My fingers join the hands they came from. My hands feel rough, and fleetingly, my old vanity returns. I want to wake up for the sole reason that I need to moisturise. But no, that is no reason to return to reality. If it does become my reason, then my old mistakes will continue. I embrace the roughness. It is a part of me, and tells its own story of life. It shows the world that I have been somewhere and it was not a nice place. It reminds me of that history.

My hands attach themselves to my forearms. Pale, covered in freckles. They belong to me alone, and they contain strength. The strength to push some people away, the strength to pull others into an embrace. The strength to know that I can do both. I can make my own choices. I promise that I will allow the right people into my space, and push the wrong people away. I will be aware of what choices I make and I will ensure they are the right choices for my daughter and I. That is my priority.

My forearms connect to my upper arms, and again the muscle shivers and writhes as though under a spell. Here is where I can love. Love doesn't come from the heart, it comes from the hug. It comes from the soul, and the soul uses the arms and hands and fingers to convey itself to others. I am beginning to feel whole. I promise that I will not allow my past to taint my future. I will learn from that past, and encompass it into my future, our future, but it will not hold us back in some kind of misery-fuelled vice.

My upper body, my chest, completes this part of the puzzle, knitting the two sections of arms and lower body into one whole piece. I feel my heart thud. I listen to each beat and remember that this is what keeps me together. It is something I almost gave up so recently, and I do not regret that, but I am glad that it fought back. This is my life. I will live it as I see fit and will no longer allow others to judge me, nor to make judgements for me. I have the body, the blood, the beat, and therefore, the right to be myself.

I see my neck, long and white, stick to my upper chest, reuniting itself with the body, giving the blood required to continue this journey to make a whole person from so many broken parts, so

199

many broken promises. There is nothing that I can be without these things. I have to remember that I am me. And that's that.

My head reforms in a pale, featureless mass. It needs the brain to become what it should be. The blood pumps up my newly attached neck, and my brain reforms. Memories rush in and around, swirling like a mass of unidentifiable colours. Slowly, and with much effort, I use these memories to make a future plan. I box them, file them, put them away, now that I have learnt all that I can from each one. I have spent months with these memories. Weeks, days, hours, minutes, seconds, each one vital. Each one the making of me. There is so much, so many. It amazes me that I have never learnt before, never realised, but perhaps I needed to stop and smell the roses. Or maybe, I needed this coma.

My ears appear on the side of my head and connect to my brain. The sounds of the hospital come through to me. Beeps, shouts, soothing noises, breathing apparatus puffing. Everything. I can hear everything. I hear Max's voice complaining about the coffee. I hear the nurse trying to placate him. I hear him complaining that he hasn't been allowed to see his child. Again, the nurse placates him. Then I hear Leanna. She is soothing Max, calming him. I feel stupendously sorry for her. There is no anger any more. She is in a lose-lose situation. If she stays with Fletcher, he will abuse her mentally, her other option is Max, who will undoubtedly abuse her physically. She is the second person I will hug, right after my Valerie.

Next, my eyes. The windows to the soul. It begins with shadows, moving and caressing each other, crossing over, separating. Then I see my eyelashes. I see them lying across my vision. My eyes, they are no longer closed, but not quite open. The light that comes from behind the lashes is painfully bright. It sears into my soul and almost makes me run back into the shadows of my existence. The coma of safety and peace, but I know now, there is no peace there, and there never will be. I try to blink, but only my lashes shift up and down in millimetres, a minuscule movement, however it does not go unnoticed.

"Did you see that?" Max says.

"See what?" A voice I only vaguely recognise, I think it must be the nurse. She deserves my thanks, my undying adoration. She has been here throughout.

"She blinked." he says

"Are you sure? I should get a doctor if you are."

"I am. She blinked."

He sounds almost angry, and I wonder why. Is it because he knows I will have much to tell when I awaken? Is it because the nurse asked him if he was sure? Is it because he thinks I might awaken with Leanna there, stood by his side? I have no idea any longer as to how his mind works, that is a part of my history that has gone, and I am glad. If I still knew how his mind worked, I may wake up with some undeniable urge to stay with him, to change him. But no, I know he is unpredictable and there is no way of changing a person who doesn't know themselves what they will do next. I've learnt this from my father, I have just never applied the knowledge before.

My eyelid is pulled up, a light of magnitudinous brightness shines into it. I can feel, physically feel, my pupil contract. The light is switched off, and as the lid closes, I glimpse Max. He looks the same. I don't know why, but I was expecting him to look dishevelled, to be somehow as affected as I am. He looks the same. The light is repeated on my other eye, and as the lid returns to its position, this time, I see the doctor. He is older, must be nearing retirement. He has a grey and ginger beard and kind, crinkled eyes. Why is it that wrinkles insinuate kindness? Perhaps it is because for a person to reach the age where wrinkles are undeniable they must have had a good life.

"Her reactions do seem to have improved."

I know that this is from the doctor due to where the voice came from rather than recognition. His words suggest he knows me, that he's been here, a part of this, for some time, but I don't remember his voice.

"Well, wake her up then." Max. Only he could be so directive.

"She'll wake up in her own time." I love the doctor.

"While you're here, when can I see my child?"

"I'm afraid there are some issues with that. When Ruth wakes up, then we'll talk to her about it. You have to understand Mr. Parker, Ruth was in a terrible state when she came in here, and we need to hear from her how that came about." I really, really love this doctor. He is a godsend.

"I've told you a thousand times that it must have happened in the accident, and if not, then I don't know where her bruises came from."

I love the way he lies. Even to authority, I can imagine his face, puce from the repressed anger, lying, lying, lying. He'll even be looking the doctor straight in the eye. It's impressive to watch. I know Leanna is still stood there, and I'm concerned that she hasn't said anything. That she hasn't told them the bruises were there before. That I was black and blue before the taxi driver even got into his car that morning.

Through the shimmer of my lashes, I can see them, well, their shapes, stood around my bed. Clustered around me as they talk out the situation. I have to make that last feature. I have to find my mouth. It is time for me to tell my side of the story, time for the truth. I imagine my lips, pink and full. Behind them are my neat white teeth, and behind that, my tongue. My mouth feels dry and deserted as it comes together. My tongue feels solid, and thick, as though it is filling my mouth with silence. I part my lips and try to poke my tongue out to wet them, to give them the lubrication they need to form the words that swim from my brain. Words are now gushing, and my tongue won't move. I cough dustily.

The conversation going on above my head ceases as though a shot has been fired.

202

"Ruth?" The doctor.

"Ruth?" The nurse.

"Sweetheart?" Max, but I hear the word overlaid. *Princess.*

"Keep him away," is all I manage to whisper, but it's enough.

"Mr. Parker, I'm pleased to say that you must now leave," the doctor says.

He does actually sound very gleeful, it's as though he's been itching to say those words for some time, and I've given him the permission he needed.

"Keep him away," I whisper again.

34.

Dear Max

How do you write what you feel? If I were an artist, I could draw emotion and pain. I could paint sound and silence, but I write and words cannot encompass the complete range I want them to, or maybe I just don't know the words I need. Is that even possible? To not know how to textualise experience? It's not as if anyone will read this. I am writing to you, but just because I write this letter does not mean I shall post it. Writing is cathartic. It can give distance for separated examination. In this instance, it cannot. The words fail me. They swim around my skull, but elude the pen in my hand. Some things are just too terrible to be written. An old cliché: too big for the page. I have to get my story down though. It's part of my recovery. It's a way of finding me. It's a way of letting you go at last.

I sit alone, Valerie is at nursery. I'm listening to beautiful, evocative guitar music played by a street busker. He seems to be ripping my soul to shreds with each note. I eat as I watch him, renewing my belief that I exist through each tender bite. Exploring my new reality with flavour as it crosses my tongue. This is something I never expected. A new life, a new place, a new me. I am no longer Ruth. I shan't tell you who I am now, I never want to be found, and so it's best this way. Valerie is still Valerie, although we share a new surname. My mother's maiden name, but I never told you what that was, so that's ok. New life, new us.

Again, rain starts to fall. People hurry away, not that it matters, I don't know who they are anyway. I stay and get wet. The cold drops soak through my shirt and my jeans, chilling me to the bone. Confirming that I have bone. This has been so much harder than I ever imagined. Recovery time for my physical self, recovery time for my mental self, the court case, the judgement, the new start.

Edinburgh. I love Edinburgh. it was the first, and the best choice. Valerie has a soft Scottish lilt already.

Finally, it is just me and the guitarist, him continuing to play in his enigmatic style. His hand over the neck, not under, beating out beauty, not strumming. Some American tourists hurry past, rushing their vacation, confirming their identity as American Tourist through their blether. Ecstatic that they have found a Hard Rock Cafe on their travels. This joy accentuated by the large Hard Rock Cafe gift bags they carry. So much baggage. Come to Edinburgh to buy a little something of life back home. One of them looks over as they pass, as if about to ask me something, then turns away muttering 'burger joint'. I must have given her my 'fuck-off' look. I deny I have one, but those closest to me these days tell me I do, and that it is quite powerful.

The Americans head off down the street, marvelling in braying, sinew-straining voices that there are shops. Yes, quite what were you expecting? I want to ask them this, but I don't. Incognito. I want to stand and scream at them. Widen their horizons to a reality that is not America nor one of its subsidiaries. That there is another world, one I'm just beginning to discover myself. I don't though, it must be a very difficult concept for them, there being so many McDonald's in this place, even so far away from their home town.

The rain begins to dissipate, and as it fades, bodies return to maraud the street. The guitar player disappears through the crowds that pass between us. Occasional snatches of his vivid red hair traverse the yards of bland crowds. More Americans. This time however, one breaks from its pack to greet a Muslim family perusing a map.

"Hey! We meet on the plane! How's your trip!"

The family appear embarrassed by this public display of vocality and comradeship, but maybe that's just me. They smile, and quietly respond to the American's deafening greeting. I know what the American is saying, It is not 'hello', it is 'look at me! I am on vacation! I can afford to come to Edinburgh!' Most importantly for me, as the disillusioned spectator to this farce, she is saying, 'Look at me! I am American and I talk to, and travel on the same planes as, Muslims!' I do not look at her. I do not watch this public display of condescension and political ideologies.

I am not anti-American, far from it, I am not even anti-anyone. I am on the road to recovery. I remember though, in the nineties, it was the done thing to be able to say, 'I am not homophobic. I have gay friends.' It was an almost global phenomenon. If you are American now, you need Muslim friends to be liberal. If you are British, you need American friends to meet the same goal. I have an American friend. He is a single Dad and his daughter is at nursery with mine. They are friends too.

I debate internally on whether or not I should approach the guitarist. At this juncture, we have no relationship aside from that of musician and audience. Performer and listener. If I approach, that magic will be gone. Yet, I want to know his name. I am beginning to meet new people now. I want to acknowledge his reality and to make it synchronise with mine. He continues to play, the other side of the narrow street, oblivious to my dilemma.

I am almost jealous of his anonymity, even though we share it. His anonymity however, is diffused by performance. People greet him and drop money into his case in front of him. I choose to blend into the surrounding. I am still scared of being found. A moment later, and I realise that there is silence. He has gone. Anonymous to me for all time, his beauty captured in my mind for all eternity. I will never know his name, but I will always know of his existence.

The wind picks up once more, and with it, comes icy rain. It is August, so this is normal for here and now. Goosebumps crawl along my arms, the hairs standing on end, but the chill revives me and reminds me that I AM. Something that these last three years, and even, the twenty odd before them, made me forget. I am recovering, like an addict, I am finding out how to live a different life.

206

It is time for me to leave this haven of voyeurism and move onto the next chapter. I pay for my food, my nourishment of my reality, and leave. I become a part of the crowd instantaneously. Catharsis. A word. Elusive. Another. Perhaps at the next moment of individual anonymity interlinked with that of another, I will find an answer, a way forward. Good luck guitarist, whoever you are, bon chance, and of course, thank you.

Once more, I crave contact. However, this time, I dream of holding someone's hand. It is a simple yet unfulfilled wish, to walk down a street, any street, mingling with the crowds, another soul at my side holding my hand. Fingers interlocking in a loving moment, a touch that contains all the information I need. That there is love, and peace, and everything. The one o'clock canon booms and it brings a smile to my face. Perhaps today will be the day. Each day is a new start and supersedes what came before.

I remember a time when I was whole and complete, when I was sixteen and the world was waiting for me. A time when I smiled with honesty and beauty, and not pain and undisguised loss. Somewhere inside me, I yearn to go back there and to change everything that happened next. Would I be the same? Would I be... me? What's done is done, the past has gone. I am a new me, it is time for me to make those first few steps, leaps even. Today is the day.

I will deal with things. I will do what I always do in times of struggle. I will re-read *Catch-22* for the umpteenth time. I will try, this time, to laugh and to cry the way I used to. Before I became numb and empty. Before I was destroyed from the top down with more effectiveness that a nuclear bomb. Or perhaps a better analogy would be that of a twin terrorist attack. At least that left shards of steel of what was once a structure. I haven't even been left with that. Perhaps this is why it seems to be so impossible for me to rebuild. I thought everything would be easy once I woke up, but it has been harder.

The Beatles song, *I wanna hold your hand*, is having a competitive discourse with the thoughts flooding through my mind. The battle is never-ending. I don't even know the words to the song, which makes it all the more perverse. The scraps of chorus fight with questions of why and how, with statements of love and hate. With the ultimate, all controlling theme of 'what next?'

I go to watch a play, and it reminds me of you, *him*, before. *The Prime of Miss Jean Brodie*. I empathised. You took me in my Prime. You had me at my best, like Teddy. I'd read the book years ago and had forgotten the pertinent points, but this performance brought it all back. Only, I wasn't assassinated by a child. A miscalculating, hurt, pained child. I was assassinated by you. You were the one that took away all that I was. You took away all that I'd lived for. There was a time when we would have seen such a play together. Discussed its finer points over a drink or two afterwards. How ironic that it was performed today in a church. A place you and I never entered together. I thank all the gods that be for small mercies.

The actors did a wonderful job, we would've found little there to criticise. So, we would've broken down the text to explore its meaning. I don't need you here to do that. I still have my intellect. Anyway, that stopped for us within the first few months of our time together. It was a hook to catch me with, no, the worm on the hook, but then there was just the hook. My love of literature and theatre are two of the few things, very few things, that you could not take from me. That and an old eighties compilation CD that I wish now I'd left with you.

A man sat next to me in the theatre, for want of a better word. He reminded me of you too. He smelt like you once did. His girlfriend had found a seat in the front row, apart from him. She turned around to check on him so many times that I was tempted to switch seats with her. He sat like you did. Effeminately. He crossed his leg over the other, reclining back in the hard wooden chair. A feat I would not have dreamed possible had I not seen it

208

with my own eyes. He was poised and spent as much time observing his girlfriend as she him. Somehow, this worried me. It also reminded me of you.

The greatest thing I took from the show, I realise as I push Valerie back to our fantastic flat in the Grassmarket, is that it is time I regained my Prime. It is not impossible, and I know how. I am going to enrol at the university tomorrow. I sent in my application and was accepted months ago, but I've been putting off enrolment. It's like I didn't want to make that final change to my life that would completely destroy all that came before. It is the one thing that is the same. I am a kept woman here still. Admittedly, kept by my own money, but I do not work, I do nothing useful. I spend my days sat in cafes and bars watching other people live their lives. It is time to live my own.

I will read Law. One day, I will work for people like me, protecting them from people like you.

Printed in Great Britain
by Amazon.co.uk, Ltd.,
Marston Gate.